RAVAGERS OF THE BORDER

OUTLAW RANGER BOOK NINE

JAMES REASONER

WOLFPACK
PUBLISHING
— EST 2013 —

Ravagers of the Border
Paperback Edition
© Copyright 2022 James Reasoner

Wolfpack Publishing
5130 S. Fort Apache Rd. 215-380
Las Vegas, NV 89148

wolfpackpublishing.com

Paperback ISBN 978-1-63977-277-3
LCCN 2021952535

Dedicated to the memory of
Michael Newton,
a fine writer and a good friend

RAVAGERS OF THE BORDER

1

LLANO GRANDE, TEXAS

EARLY MORNING LIKE THIS WAS THE ONLY TIME THE AIR
really felt decent here in South Texas. By nine o'clock it
would start to get hot, and by ten, men would be sleeving
sweat off their foreheads and ladies would be fanning
themselves in a futile effort to dry the "glow" from their
faces—because everybody knew that ladies didn't
perspire, and they damn sure didn't sweat.

But at seven o'clock, the air still held a hint of coolness, especially when the breeze blew from the east,
where the Gulf of Mexico lay sixty miles away. Bert
Jennings, marshal of the small town of Llano Grande,
stepped out onto the porch of the Rio Café, where he
had just enjoyed breakfast, and drew in a deep breath,
enjoying the freshness of it. He hooked his thumbs in the
pockets of his vest and reflected that life wasn't too bad,
although as a widower, he missed his wife Inez. The grief
was still sharp sometimes, since she'd only been gone a

year, but mostly it was just a dull ache. He had learned to live with that.

Jennings was ready to stroll up the street to the marshal's office when he stiffened and frowned. From where he stood, he could look diagonally across the street and see a short distance into the alley between the First State Bank of Llano Grande and Fernandez's Hardware Store. The sun wasn't high enough in the sky to penetrate very far into the shadows of that alley, but it was bright enough for Jennings to see a flicker of movement in the gloom.

Nobody had any business being in that alley at this time of day. The hardware store wouldn't open for another hour yet, and it would be almost two hours before Roberto Ruiz, the president of the bank, would toddle along the boardwalk and unlock the front door.

Jennings squinted, trying to make out what he was looking at. The thing in the alley was there, then it was gone, then it was there again, flipping in and out of his sight.

That was a dadgum horse's tail jerking around in there, Jennings realized. He was looking at the back end of a horse. But what was it doing in that alley next to the bank?

The most likely answer wasn't anything good.

Jennings frowned and started across the street. Not many folks were moving around yet. The other way up the street, a wagon creaked and rattled toward Dugan's livery stable and blacksmith shop. Somebody getting their team reshod. Off a ways, a dog barked. A woman's voice called in sharp Spanish, yelling at a kid. Nothing unusual going on.

Jennings heard hooves stomping nervously in the alley ahead of him. It wasn't just one horse in there, but several. He wrapped his hand around the butt of the Colt holstered on his right hip as he edged sideways to get a better look.

The bank had a side door that opened into the alley, he recalled. But it was thick, had a sturdy lock as well as a bar across it inside, and was hardly ever opened. It was a way into the bank, though, if somebody was determined enough.

He was close enough now to see a cluster of half a dozen horses, at least, with a man standing in the shadows holding their reins. The man hadn't pulled them far enough into the alley to keep Jennings from spotting the last one's tail as it flicked flies away.

Beyond the horse-holder stood several other men, all of them wearing steeple-crowned sombreros and long coats like the man with the reins. They were gathered around something, but suddenly they pulled back from it and hurried toward the street, practically running.

At the same instant, the horse-holder turned his head and spotted Jennings trying to slip up on him. The man yelled a warning in Spanish. He jerked his gun out. So did Jennings. They fired at each other across the backs of the horses.

A small explosion—more of a heavy thump, really—sounded at the same time as the pair of shots. Smoke roiled in the alley. That was dynamite, Jennings thought wildly. They'd blown the bank's side door open!

He ran to his left, immediately breathing hard, cursing his age and the big breakfast he'd just eaten. As the echoes from the explosion faded, he heard more shots. None of them hit him, so he was thankful for that. He reached the water barrel he'd been running toward and dropped into a crouch behind it. Similar barrels were spaced along the street at intervals, ready for use in case a fire ever broke out.

The bank and another building were between this barrel and the alley mouth. Jennings stuck his gun over the top of it and triggered a pair of shots in the alley's general direction, without actually aiming. As he leaned against the barrel, he felt it shiver from the impact of bullets striking it. Water would be leaking out of it now, Jennings knew, and if the level dropped enough, those bullets might start coming all the way through.

Men shouted, and another muffled explosion shook the ground under his feet. Now the bandits had blown the door off the vault, he figured. And there was no way he could stop them by himself, outnumbered at least six to one. He'd be lucky to live through this unexpected violence.

But it was his job to try to stop them. He steeled himself, willing his muscles to work and lift him so he could better direct his shots toward the lawbreakers.

With a clatter of hoofbeats, the gang burst out of the alley, mounted now. They sprayed shots toward the barrel just as Bert Jennings rose from behind it. He felt the crash of a slug against his body and toppled over backward. The bullet had hit him somewhere on the left side. He didn't pass out, didn't drop his gun. He struggled to lift it as the bank robbers galloped past him. He saw that they had black masks over their faces, so only a narrow strip for their eyes was left uncovered between the masks and the pulled-down sombreros. One of them shouted a curse at him in Spanish, thrust a gun toward him, and snapped off a couple of shots. They struck the water barrel and chewed splinters from it, splinters that stung Jennings' freshly shaven cheeks. He got off one more shot, and then they were past him, thundering out

4

of town with whatever loot they had gotten from the bank.

It sure had happened in a hurry, he thought as he gasped in pain, laid his gun down, and reached across his body to press his right hand against the hot, wet spot on his left side where owlhoot lead had gouged into him.

———

BERT JENNINGS SHIFTED in the bed, trying to find a comfortable position. That wasn't really possible, though, when a fella had been shot and had bandages wrapped so tightly around him that he could barely breathe.

He was in the back room of Dr. Joseph Lawlor's house, the room that Doc Lawlor kept for patients who needed continuing care while they recuperated. The peppery little medico had declared that Jennings would be flat on his back for at least three weeks recovering from the gunshot wound he had suffered while battling the bank robbers. Jennings knew there was no way he was going to lay around that long, but for now, at least, he was too weak to do much of anything else.

Voices sounded from the front of the house where Lawlor's examination rooms and surgery were located. Jennings couldn't make out the words, but he figured from Lawlor's tone, the doc was telling somebody they couldn't come back here. It didn't do any good, because a moment later heavy footsteps clomped down the hallway. Simon Dugan stuck his shaggy-haired, walrus-mustached face in the door.

Llano Grande's blacksmith and part-time, unofficial, volunteer deputy marshal wore a doleful expression. He shook his head and said, "They got away, Bert. Sorry."

JAMES REASONER

Before Doc Lawlor had knocked him out with chloroform so he could extract the bullet that was still in Jennings' side, the marshal had been alert enough to send for Dugan and order him to form a posse and go after the robbers. Dugan had agreed. Jennings hadn't seen him again until now, quite a few hours later.

With a sigh, Jennings said, "I was afraid of that. What happened, Simon?"

"That bunch didn't try to hide their tracks. We were able to follow 'em all the way to the Rio Grande. We got after 'em in a hurry, too. Caught up enough to spot the varmints on the other side." Dugan looked grim. "I got half a mind to think they were waitin' for us. Thievin' varmints took off their sombreros and waved 'em in the air and yipped and hollered, just tauntin' us that they was on the other side of the border and there wasn't a damn thing we could do about it."

"You didn't go after them, did you?"

Dugan's big hands clenched into fists and then opened a few times. "I wanted to," he rumbled. "In the old days, I reckon I would have. But that's Old Mexico over there, and we wouldn't have had any legal standin' if we crossed the river. I couldn't risk all those boys who rode with me gettin' into trouble over it."

Jennings nodded and said, "You did the right thing."

"But Bert, they blowed the door off the vault in the bank and got all the money that was in there! A lot of folks are plumb wiped out! There's got to be somethin' we can do."

"There is. Go to the telegraph office and send a wire to Austin." Jennings' jaw tightened. "Tell the Rangers we need help down here on the border, and we need it pronto!"

2

RANCHO DEL HALCON

RODRIGO CABAL YAWNED SO BIG IT FELT LIKE HIS JAW WAS going to crack wide open. At the same time, the young vaquero stretched both arms wide and arched his back, easing muscles grown stiff from a long night in the saddle. Dawn was not far off now. Already a band of reddish gold was visible on the eastern horizon, a harbinger of the sun that would soon rise. And when it did, Rodrigo's turn on nighthawk duty would be over. One of the other vaqueros who rode for the Rancho del Halcon would relieve him and he could head back to the bunk house for some sleep.

The herd was an irregular black shape that sprawled across a large tract of land not far from the Rio Bravo. The vaqueros who rode for Don Abraham Ordóñez, lord of the Rancho del Halcon, had been combing the range for a week now, gathering this herd. It was ready to be driven down the Rio Bravo to Matamoros, where it would be sold. Don Abraham would grow richer. The vaqueros would not, but it had never been a vaquero's fate to grow rich. The wise ones knew this and contented themselves with the knowledge that they lived free, rode good horses, had the friendship of fine amigos, the occasional company of a beautiful—or at least willing—woman, and a bottle of tequila from time to time. It was a good life for a young man, Rodrigo reflected as he drew in his arms from his stretching yawn.

The rifle bullet that struck him in the back, ripped through his body, nicked his heart, and burst out his chest ended that life with no warning.

As if the shot that killed Rodrigo Cabal has been a signal to throw wide the gates of hell, at least half a dozen riders loomed out of the dawn, charging toward the herd as clouds of dust coiled up from the hooves of their galloping mounts. Orange tongues of flame stabbed from the muzzles of their guns as they opened fire on the other vaqueros tending to the herd. The gunfire spooked the cattle. The beasts lurched out of their night-time stupor and, like one gigantic organism, surged toward the Rio Bravo, about a mile away.

One vaquero survived the attack, although he was shot twice, once in the shoulder and once through the body. Diego Garrido was found later by Don Abraham and more of his riders and taken to the hacienda to be nursed back to health by the women.

"The men who attacked us were gringos, Don Abraham," Garrido told the rancher when he regained consciousness. "I saw them. They wore long coats and big hats, like the Texas devils wear, and they had masks on their faces. I heard them shouting and cursing in English as they killed your men and stampeded your cattle toward the river."

"Rest, Diego," Don Abraham said as he squeezed a hand on the vaquero's uninjured shoulder. "We will find these men and make them pay for what they have done."

But the killers and the cattle they had stolen were gone, vanished across the Rio Bravo—what the *Norte Americanos* called the Rio Grande—into Texas.

ESPERANZA

George Washington Braddock Jr.—who went by G.W. and *never* "Junior"—stretched his long legs out in front of him and crossed them at the ankles. His arms were crossed on his chest, and his head was tipped forward so that his hat brim shaded his eyes. He was sitting on a bench in front of the village's church. The dignified adobe building with its small bell tower loomed behind him, a peaceful backdrop in the middle of the day when heat drove most of the village's inhabitants inside for *siesta*.

Braddock wasn't asleep, though, or even dozing. He was wide awake because, a moment earlier, he had heard bare feet slapping rapidly against the dirt and the huffing and puffing of someone running in the midday sun. From under the lowered hat brim, Braddock's narrowed eyes watched the figure that appeared out of the heat haze, hurrying toward him.

With a sigh, Braddock uncrossed his arms, pulled in his legs, and unfolded upward off the bench, a tall, lean man whose graceful movements barely hinted at his speed and power. He thumbed his hat back, revealing a deeply tanned face with a scar on his forehead running up into his thick, sandy brown hair.

The stocky villager came to a stop in front of Braddock and leaned over to rest his hands on his thighs as he tried to catch his breath. Braddock asked, "What is it, Tomás?"

Tomás wheezed a time or two, then waved a hand toward the north. "A rider, he comes, señor Braddock. From Texas."

"From the direction of the border, you mean. You don't know he comes from Texas."

"He is a gringo and has the big hat, señor! And he rides as if he owns the entire world and is generous enough to allow the rest of us to live in it. If he is not a Texan, he is pretending to be, and doing a good job of it!"

Braddock had to chuckle at that, which relieved the naturally grim cast to his features for a moment. He was a Texan his own self, born, bred, and forever, but he could understand why some people not lucky enough to be from the Lone Star State felt the way they did about it.

Not that he was overly sentimental about Texas, after what the legislature had done a few years earlier, gutting the Texas Rangers and taking his badge away from him, along with those carried by many other good men, all over something as useless and ephemeral as politics.

"Whoever he is, whatever he wants, I'll take care of it, Tomás," Braddock said. "Don't worry about it."

The people of Esperanza had come to regard him as their protector, even though he was often away from the village for long stretches of time. He had saved them from outlaws and vicious *rurales*, and they would never forget that.

"Gracias, señor Braddock." Tomás huffed and puffed some more and then sank onto the bench. "I believe . . . I will sit down . . . for a few minutes."

"You do that. Thanks for letting me know."

Braddock didn't get in any hurry as he strolled toward the cantina at the other end of the street. By the time he got there and leaned casually against the hitch rail in front of the building, the rider was only a couple of hundred yards away. As Tomás had said, he wore a big hat and carried himself with a self-confidence that bordered on arrogance. Braddock continued standing out in the open. His instincts told him this stranger had come to Esperanza looking for him.

The man rode straight on until he stopped and pulled his horse around so that he faced Braddock squarely. "G.W.," he said. "Been a long time."

"That it has," Braddock agreed. "You're out of your bailiwick, John Edward. What are you doing down here?"

"Looking for you," replied Texas Ranger John Edward Slattery. He glanced around the village. "Why else would I come to a pest hole like this?"

Braddock bristled inside. Esperanza might not be much, but it was the closest thing to a home he had these days. Keeping his expression and his voice neutral, he inclined his head toward the cantina's entrance and invited, "Come on in and have a drink. You can tell me what it's all about."

A faint smile tugged at Slattery's mouth. "No reason not to, seeing as we're south of the border and I don't have any official standing here."

"Not that official standing ever kept a Ranger from quenching his thirst when he needed to."

"No, not very often."

Braddock straightened away from the hitch rail. Slattery swung down from the saddle, looped his reins around the rail, and followed Braddock into the cantina's shadowy interior.

It was too hot for tequila, so Braddock settled for beer and Slattery did likewise. The cantina's other customers watched from the corners of their eyes as the two Texans settled down at a table in a rear corner. The tall gringos seemed friendly enough, so evidently gunplay wasn't about to break out. The other men in the place kept a wary eye on them anyway. You never could tell when Texans would decide to shoot each other for some reason, real or imagined.

Braddock took a sip of his beer and asked quietly, "Have you come to arrest me, John Edward? Bend a gun barrel over my head and drag me back across the border?"

Slattery said, "Hmmph. What kind of damn fool do you think I am? A lot of us who are still carrying badges thought it was a crying shame what the politicians did to you and others like you. You were one of the finest Rangers in the outfit. You never should have been let go like that." Slattery swallowed some beer, licked his lips, and went on, "Of course, that didn't give you the right to go around pretending to still be a Ranger and sticking your nose into our business. It made you some enemies when word got around about that."

Braddock shrugged, the depth of his indifference eloquently expressed in the rise and fall of his shoulders. "I'm a lawman, John Edward. All I've ever been, all I'll ever be. Whether or not I carry a badge doesn't change that." He smiled. "Anyway, *I* still pack the circle star, too."

He slipped slim, supple fingers into a hidden pocket on the back of his broad gunbelt. With a flick of his wrist, he tossed the object he pulled out onto the table in front of Slattery, who looked at it and grunted.

The thing was a Texas Ranger badge, the famous silver star set inside a silver circle, fashioned out of a Mexican coin. In the center of it was a small, neat hole, left by a bullet.

"Legally, that doesn't count for anything," said Slattery.

"It's the only authority I need," Braddock said. He picked up the badge and stowed it away out of sight again. "I notice you're not wearing one."

Slattery patted the breast pocket of his shirt. "Took it off and put it away when I crossed the Rio. Figured that down here it might be more of a target than anything else."

"You might not be far wrong," Braddock conceded. "Mexico's a pretty volatile place these days. Lots of bands of revolutionaries roaming around. Some of them . . . a few of them . . . actually just want what's best for the country. For the rest, it's just a good excuse to loot and kill their enemies while shouting *Viva le revolución!*" He drank more of the beer. "President Diaz doesn't like that, so he's got the *rurales* combing the countryside for them."

"Said *rurales* being little more than bandits themselves."

Braddock inclined his head. "Mostly true. The moral of the story is that it's easy to get yourself shot down here these days, whether you're a gringo or not."

"You seem to do all right."

"They're used to me by now," Braddock said dryly.

"Well, I don't intend to stay down here south of the border for long. I have work to do on the other side of the river, and I thought maybe you could give me a hand with it."

"Ah, now we're getting to the reason why you're here.

You want me to come back to Texas and help you with a case? Are you offering me my job back, John Edward?"

"I would if I could, you know that, but . . . no. What I want you to do is on this side of the Rio, where I don't have any jurisdiction."

"That didn't always stop the Rangers in the past."

"We're a little pickier about following the law these days," Slattery said. "Captain Hughes keeps an eye on us, because the politicians keep an eye on him. He doesn't want to give those vultures any excuse to disband the Rangers completely and permanently."

Braddock nodded and said, "I can understand that. What's the case?"

"Some gang has been raising hell up and down the Rio Grande for a spell. They've hit banks in Brownsville, Rio Grande City, Llano Grande, and several other towns. They've held up stagecoaches, and they've run off stock from half a dozen ranches." Bleak lines appeared on Slattery's weathered face. "In the process, they've also killed close to a dozen people, including two women and a kid. They're not careful about throwing lead around when anybody tries to stop them."

Braddock's expression was grim, too. "Same bunch every time?"

"The description's the same. Dusters and sombreros and masks over their faces, and the outlaws always talk to each other in Spanish. Posse's have chased them to the Rio, but they have to stop there when the gang crosses into Mexico. From the reports I've heard, they're a high-handed bunch. They wave their hats in the air and yell back across the river at the posse's before they ride off."

"Making fun of them?"

"Yeah. They ride off before anybody can get a shot at them."

14

"So everybody thinks they're Mexican *bandidos*."

Slattery's eyebrows lifted in apparent surprise at Braddock's tone. "You don't?"

"I don't have a clue in the world if they are or not," Braddock said. "But anybody can put on a sombrero and yell in Spanish."

"I reckon that's true. But whoever is under those masks, they're hiding out down here in Mexico. Cap'n Hughes wants me to find out who they are and where they're going to hit next, so he can have enough Rangers waiting there to put a stop to their little fandangos."

"Sounds like a tall order," Braddock commented. He had a pretty good idea what Slattery was going to say next.

"Yeah, but it'd be a lot easier if I could get a hand from somebody working on this side of the line. Somebody who knows the ground and can sort of blend in because . . ."

"Because he's an outlaw himself?"

Slattery shook his head. "I didn't say that, G.W. I don't think there's a man in the Rangers who truly considers you an outlaw. That's why we've left you alone whenever you've come back into Texas to work as a . . . well, as a hired gun."

Braddock shrugged again and didn't deny the characterization. He hadn't really liked some of the jobs he'd done, but a man had to eat. And some of the money he'd earned had gone back into helping folks here in Esperanza.

Slattery went on, "There are rumors that you were mixed up in that ugly business up at *Isla de Cordoba* not long ago, too, helping out the Rangers there."

"Yeah, well, that didn't play out the way one particular Ranger hoped."

Slattery held up his hands, palms out. "I don't need to hear anything about that. It's over and done with. My only concern is finding those snakes and putting a stop to their looting and killing. What do you say, G.W.? Can I count on you?"

Braddock looked out through the cantina's open doorway and along Esperanza's single street. Nothing was moving except a dog slinking across the street, probably bound for a shady spot under a porch where he could doze the afternoon away. If he wasn't careful, Braddock mused, he might turn into the same sort of creature.

"I'll see what I can do," he told Slattery.

3

A week later, Braddock nudged his dun horse through a gap between two rock-studded ridges. The hair on the back of his neck was standing up. It had been ever since he'd started through the narrow passage. If what his gut was telling him was right, trouble might be waiting at the other end.

Not for the first time in the past week, he asked himself why he had agreed to help John Edward Slattery. It wasn't like the two of them were old friends or anything like that. They had been acquainted when Braddock was an actual Ranger, but that was the extent of it.

Come to think of it, though, Braddock hadn't had any really close friends among the Rangers, maybe because he had been so focused on his job, on carrying out his duties, on living up to his father's legacy. There hadn't been time to forge any close relationships. Not while there were outlaws to bring to justice.

But since he had given Slattery his word, Braddock

had no choice except to follow through on that pledge. Slattery had returned to Texas to tackle the assignment on that side of the border. Braddock had packed some supplies, said his farewells to the mission priest and a few others in Esperanza, and headed southeast on the dun, paralleling the Rio Grande. Texas was a big place, and it had taken a long ride for him to reach his destination.

By now he ought to be getting into the area where the elusive outlaw gang was operating. That knowledge might be making him a little more wary. It never hurt to be careful. Plenty of hombres who never learned that lesson had crossed the divide early.

Braddock thought about sliding the Winchester under his right leg from its sheath and carrying it across the saddle in front of him. But if it came down to gun work when he emerged from this gap, more than likely the range would be fairly short, he reasoned, so he left the rifle where it was and told himself that he'd rely on the Colt.

Sure enough, as he rode out of the passage, the riders who quickly closed in on him from both sides crowded up, well within handgun range. However, they hadn't pulled their irons, so he kept his right hand resting lightly on his thigh, ready to draw but not making any aggressive moves . . . yet.

"Hold it right there, hombre!" one of the men called to him in Spanish. After years on the border, Braddock was as fluent in that tongue as he was in English. He brought the dun to a stop.

There had been two men behind each bluff. They worked it now so they surrounded him, the one in front of him who had spoken, one on each side, and one drifting around behind him. If they meant to kill him, he probably wouldn't be able to keep them from doing it, but he was confident he could take at least two of them with him.

They didn't act like they wanted to gun him down, at least not yet. No doubt they wanted to find out first who he was and what he was doing here.

Their rough, patched clothes, stained and battered sombreros, and the coiled reatas on their saddles told him they were vaqueros and probably not outlaws. Bandidos generally dressed better. There was no guarantee his assessment was correct, Braddock reminded himself, but he had a hunch these weren't any of the men he was looking for. They seemed more curious than hostile.

"You are on the wrong side of the border, eh, gringo?" The spokesman grinned as he asked the question.

"Not necessarily," Braddock replied. "Sometimes a man is no longer welcome in his homeland. I'm told there are a lot of former Texans who have gotten their feet wet in the Rio Grande."

That made the vaquero laugh. "This is true," he admitted. "There are too many of you over here now, and most are up to no good." The smile on his hard-planed face went away. "What are you doing on the Rancho del Halcon?"

"Ranch of the Hawk, eh? Named after the owner?"

The vaquero stiffened even more. "Don Abraham Ordóñez owns this range. It has been in the Ordóñez family for many generations, ever since it was granted to them by the King of Spain more than two hundred years ago!"

Braddock nodded and said, "I meant no disrespect to

Don Abraham. I believe I've heard of him. Supposed to be a good man."

"He is," the vaquero snapped. "And as such, he does not deserve what has happened."

Braddock shrugged. "Been my experience that folks hardly ever get what they deserve. Most of the time, that's unfortunate. But some are downright lucky that they don't."

"Never mind about that." The vaquero finally made a threatening move. He put his hand on the butt of his gun. So did the other men. "Answer my question, gringo. Quickly."

"My name is Braddock. I mean no harm to your boss or his ranch. I'm just one hombre passing through. Not much I could really do to cause trouble, is there?"

"One never knows. What is your destination?"

"Whatever's that way." Braddock nodded in front of him.

"The town of Los Pinos?"

Braddock laughed. "Are there really any pine trees in this border country? Plenty of them over in East Texas, and farther west in the mountains of the Big Bend, but I don't recall ever seeing any in this part of the world."

"The man who founded Los Pinos was from the mountains farther south in Mexico," the vaquero explained. "He missed the trees of his homeland and planted some, but they did not live. The name is all that remains. Such is the legend, anyway." He scowled. "It does not matter. I do not trust you, señor. You are not welcome on the Rancho del Halcon. You will not have the chance to add to our troubles."

"What troubles?" Braddock shook his head. "I don't know anything about what may have happened here."

The man to his right spoke up, blurting out, "Our amigos died! Died at the hands of gringos like you!"

He started to draw his gun.

"Pablo, no!" the spokesman cried. He flung out a hand in an urgent gesture. "Stop!"

The vaquero who had tried to draw had his pistol halfway out of its holster. But Braddock's heavy Colt was all the way out and leveled, having appeared in his hand in a blur of motion that was almost supernatural. His thumb was looped over the hammer, holding it back.

Pablo let go of his gun butt like it was hot and allowed the revolver to sag back into its holster.

"You boys can shoot me if you want," Braddock told the other men, "but if you do, Pablo here is going to die when I let go of this hammer. I didn't come here looking for trouble, but I don't intend to die quietly, either."

"No one is going to shoot you, señor Braddock," the spokesman said. "Put your gun away."

"All four of you move around where I can see you," Braddock responded. "Then I'll think about it."

The spokesman barked orders. He and the other two nudged their horses into motion and shifted around to join Pablo where Braddock could cover all of them at once. They directed sullen glares at him. He lowered the Colt's hammer but kept it pointed at them.

"I don't know what happened here," he said, "but I didn't have anything to do with it. Right now, is the first time I've ever been on your Don Abraham's range. Why don't you tell me what it is that's got you hombres so riled up?"

"A month ago, eight of our compadres died, shot down by thieves who stole a herd we had gathered so it could be driven to Matamoros and sold. They attacked at dawn, shooting our friends in the back like the cowards they are!"

"What did they do with the herd?"

"Stampeded it across the river into Texas, of course. What else would gringos do with it?"

"You seem pretty sure it was gringos who were responsible," Braddock commented.

The spokesman for the vaqueros snorted. "One of our men survived the raid, although he will never be the same after being wounded so badly. He saw them with their big Stetson hats and heard them shouting orders to each other in English. He said they wore masks, but he knew them for what they were. And later, when the rest of us followed the tracks of the stolen cattle, they led straight to the Rio Bravo and across into Texas. We could see where the herd left the river."

"Tell him about the men on the other side," urged Pablo, who looked as angry and on the verge of losing control as ever. The memory of how fast and slick Braddock pulled iron made him keep a tight rein on his emotions, though.

"There were men waiting for us," the spokesman said, "as if they knew we would follow the herd there. They sat on the other side of the river, at the edge of the chaparral. They took their hats off and waved them in the air, laughing. We shot at them, of course, but not in time. They darted back into the chaparral and disappeared . . . still laughing." The vaquero drew in a deep breath. "We wanted to go after them, even then, but Don Abraham ordered us not to cross the border. He would have dared it for himself, but he would not allow his men to risk getting into that much trouble."

Braddock nodded slowly. "That's an interesting yarn. Seems like I've heard something similar to it lately."

"I would not be surprised, señor. Rancho del Halcon is not the only place where these gringo raiders have struck. They have stolen stock from other ranches and attacked several towns, robbing the banks, looting other businesses, and then fleeing across the Rio Bravo. They are devils, señor."

"Texas devils!" added Pablo.

"Well, that may be," Braddock said, "but I'm not one of them. I'm sorry to hear about your troubles—"

"That is not all," the vaquero interrupted. "Several more of our men have been shot from ambush in the past month. Two were killed, the others badly wounded."

"And gringos did that, too?" Braddock asked with a wry tone in his voice.

"Who else?" Pablo responded hotly. "No one else would do such an evil thing!"

The other vaquero said, "No one has seen these hidden killers, but what Pablo says is true. It must be the same men. Their lawlessness spreads all the way down the valley to the Gulf of Mexico."

"You said they've robbed banks. Is there one in Los Pinos?"

The vaquero looked a little surprised by the question, but he nodded and said, "Yes, there is, and it was robbed two weeks ago."

"Must have been quite a blow to Don Abraham, to lost that herd and then such a short time later lose whatever money he had in the bank. If he actually *did* have any money in the bank?"

"He did," snapped the vaquero. "Not that it is any business of yours."

"No, I suppose it's not," Braddock said. "I'm just curious because, like I told you, I'm new in this country. Sort of like to know what's going on in a place, so I can decide whether I want to stay a spell or twirl my twine and move on."

"You would do best to move on," the vaquero advised. "Because of what has happened, gringos are less welcome than ever on this side of the border."

"I'll bear that in mind," Braddock said. "I expect when the four of you spotted me riding alone, you figured me for one of those bushwhackers you talked about."

"It seemed a likely possibility."

"I'm glad you didn't just shoot me out of hand, then." A smile tugged at the corners of Braddock's mouth. "I expect ol' Pablo there wanted to."

Pablo was about to make some retort when the spokesman lifted a hand to silence him. The man nodded to the north and said, "The border is that way, less than a mile. An easy ride. You would do well to be on the other side of the Rio Bravo before nightfall, señor."

Still smiling, Braddock said, "You may think so, but I have my doubts about that, amigo. I've been on a long trail. I crave some hot food and a real bed with a roof over my head. I think I'll check out this Los Pinos town you mentioned."

"You will be sorry, señor."

"Won't be the first time, if that little prediction comes true. Now, you can trail along with me while I cross your boss's ranch, if you want, just to see for yourselves that I'm not up to any mischief . . . or you can toss your guns away and get down off those horses so I can haze them off far enough you won't be able to catch up to me. The choice is yours."

"How dare you!" Pablo burst out. "There are still four of us and one of you—"

"And my gun's out and yours aren't," Braddock interrupted coolly. "Well, amigos, what's it going to be?"

The spokesman suddenly smiled and said, "Neither, I believe." He nodded as if to indicate something behind Braddock.

"Now, you don't expect me to—"

Braddock stopped short as he heard the swift rata-plan of hoofbeats coming through the gap between the ridges.

4

Braddock pulled the dun halfway around so he could still see the four vaqueros from the corner of his left eye, but at the same time he was able to catch a glimpse of the group of seven or eight riders pounding through the gap toward him.

He didn't have time to gather any more than an impression of the newcomers: most of them were the same sort of working vaqueros as the men he had already encountered. But the two riders in the forefront were better dressed, rode better horses, and had flashier saddles.

Then a new threat jerked his attention back to the first group. Pablo lunged his horse at Braddock, shouting, "Shoot me now, if you dare, gringo!"

Caught between two forces like this, Braddock knew he wouldn't make it out of here if he opened fire. But Pablo wasn't slowing down, so Braddock rammed his Colt back in its holster and turned the dun to be more prepared for the man's attack.

Pablo launched himself from his saddle in an attempt

to tackle Braddock and bear him to the ground. Braddock jerked his mount aside. Pablo missed and sprawled in the dirt in an ungainly heap.

A voice rang out from the newcomers as they swept up. "Get that man! Pull him off his horse!"

The clear, strong tones in which the orders were given surprised Braddock enough to freeze him for a second. They belonged to a woman.

That second was enough of a distraction for the other vaqueros to reach him and lay hands on him. As they grabbed him, one of their horses rammed a shoulder into Braddock's dun. The collision made both mounts go down. As his horse was falling, Braddock kicked his feet free of the stirrups and threw his legs out so he wouldn't be pinned.

That didn't help him with the vaqueros. Two of them had hold of his arms. Another tackled him around the thighs and held him down. He couldn't fight back as the fourth man began slugging punches into his body.

Braddock had only one weapon left. He twisted his shoulders, craned his neck, and leaned his head to the side to sink his teeth into the wrist of one of the vaqueros holding him. The man howled at the sudden, unexpected pain and let go of Braddock's left arm as he jerked his hand back. Braddock tasted blood in his mouth.

With one arm free, Braddock shot that fist up into the chin of the man kneeling on his midsection and hammering him with punches. The blow landed solidly as the man was spewing curses at Braddock and caused his teeth to close hard on his tongue. Blood spurted between the man's lips, along with a strangled cry.

Braddock bucked his body up and threw the man off. He rolled onto his side and hooked a fist into the belly of the man holding his right arm. Instead of letting go, the man wrapped his arms tighter around Braddock's arm, hunched his back, drove with his knees, and slammed the top of his head into Braddock's jaw. A wave of red-streaked blackness threatened to wash over Braddock's brain.

Braddock clung desperately to consciousness and thrust the ball of his left hand under the vaquero's chin. He levered the man's head back with a hard shove. The vaquero had to let go or risk Braddock breaking his neck.

That just left the man holding Braddock's legs. Braddock jackknifed the upper half of his body and slammed his cupped hands against the man's ears. The man yelled in a mixture of pain and anger and let go of Braddock's legs to clap his hands over his injured ears. Braddock jerked his right leg up and crashed a boot heel into the man's chest in a powerful kick that threw him backward.

Free of the vaqueros now, Braddock rolled to his right. Clouds of dust kicked up by horses' hooves swirled around him, clogging his throat and nose and stinging his eyes. A massive shape loomed up, almost on top of him, and he had to throw himself desperately to the side to avoid being trampled by one of the riders.

Braddock had to keep rolling as more hooves pounded down around him. The woman shouted, "Filthy gringo! How dare you!"

How dare he do *what?* Braddock wondered. Fight back to save his life? Did that loco woman think that he ought to just give up and let them kill him?

He didn't have time to ponder the questions. He managed to put some space between himself and the rider bent on trampling him and surged to his feet. The rider who'd been after him was the woman. No surprise there, considering how she'd acted so far.

As Braddock came upright, another rider crowded in behind him. Something struck him a slashing blow across the back that made him take a couple of stumbling steps forward. He looked over his shoulder and realized that one of the men had hit him with a coiled rata. The man was coming in again, the rope swinging toward Braddock's head.

He ducked under it, reached up, and caught hold of the man's sleeve. He heaved as hard as he could. The man came out of the saddle, yelled in alarm, and crashed down on his back with enough force to leave him stunned.

Through the roiling dust, Braddock saw the expensive clothes and knew the man he had unhorsed was one of the riders he had seen in the forefront of the second group. Dressed like that, he had to be a man of some importance. Braddock reached for his holster, but the Colt wasn't there anymore. It had slipped out during the fracas, and he didn't figure he had time to look for it.

But the man on the ground at his feet was packing a revolver in a holster with a military flap on it. Moving fast, Braddock bent, unsnapped the flap's fastener, and straightened with the gun in his hand. He thought that if he threatened the man he had taken it from, the others might pull back for the moment. There was a chance that hombre was their boss, Don Abraham Ordóñez, and even if he wasn't, he was bound to be somebody important.

Before Braddock could put that plan into action, the woman lunged her horse alongside him and brought down a quirt that slashed across the back of his hand, drawing blood. The vicious blow made his fingers open involuntarily. The gun slipped out of his grip and thudded to the ground. Braddock had to twist aside as the woman tried to rip his face open with a backhanded swipe of the quirt.

She rode astride, wearing tight black trousers tucked into high-topped black boots. Braddock got hold of her left leg and jerked it upward. With a startled cry, the woman tumbled out of the saddle on the far side.

Braddock adjusted his plan. Now he wanted to get his hands on her. With her as his prisoner, the men would have no choice but to give up their attack on him.

Once again, the odds were stacked too high against him. One of the vaqueros from the second group dived from his saddle and tackled Braddock from behind. The impact knocked Braddock off his feet. He landed face down, with the vaquero's weight on his back driving him against the ground. That forced the air out of his lungs and left him stunned and helpless.

"Hang on to him, you fools!" the woman shrieked. "Get him on his feet!"

Strong hands, too many of them for Braddock to have any chance of fighting back, closed cruelly around his arms and lifted him. His captors set him on his feet and held him tightly. This time there would be no escape.

The woman had picked herself up from the ground where she had fallen when Braddock unhorsed her. She stalked toward him, the quirt hissing in the air as she slashed it back and forth in front of her.

Her hat had come off, freeing thick masses of black, wavy hair that flowed like a midnight river around her shoulders. She wore a white shirt with an embroidered vest over it. The elaborate stitchery formed a red rose on each side of the vest that lifted and fell with the motion of her breasts as she breathed hard. Her shirt was unbuttoned at the throat, causing the garment to gape open enough to reveal a smooth expanse of honey-colored skin. Dark brown eyes flashed in her heart-shaped face. Her lips were as naturally red as the embroidered crimson flowers on her vest. She was beautiful, no doubt about that, and even a man in a predicament like Braddock's current one couldn't help but see that.

Those flashing eyes were full of fury, though, and the crimson lips twisted with hate as she cried, "I'll teach the damned gringo to hurt our people! I'll cut him to ribbons!"

With that quirt she was wielding, she might well have been able to do that. She drew back her arm, and Braddock could tell she intended to slash him in the face. A few such blows would probably blind him.

Then a gun crashed somewhere nearby, and the young woman stopped with the quirt still poised behind her head.

"Rosalita!" The voice that called out following the shot was deep and powerful. "Stop that and step away from that man."

Braddock could still turn his head. That was the only part of his body he could move. He did so, and now that the dust was clearing up some, he was able to see three more riders approaching.

One rode slightly ahead of the other two. He sat tall and straight in the saddle, despite the age to which his white, spade-shaped beard testified. He held a revolver with smoke still curling from the muzzle, so Braddock knew he had fired the shot.

As the white-bearded man reined to a stop a few feet away, the clean lines of his face and his dignified demeanor made him look like a Spanish grandee from two centuries earlier. The obvious deference the vaqueros showed him told Braddock he was looking at Don Abraham Ordóñez.

That meant the younger man he had taken the gun away from earlier wasn't the owner of this rancho. Ordóñez's son, perhaps. Braddock thought he saw a family resemblance as the younger man, sputtering with anger, picked himself up from the ground.

"But, Papa," the young woman objected as she finally lowered the quirt, "this man is one of the gringos who stole our cattle and killed our men!"

"And how do you know this, Rosalita?" asked Ordónèz.

"He is on our range. Who else could he be?"

"Maybe an innocent traveler who knows nothing of your family's troubles?" Braddock suggested in Spanish. That was stretching the truth a mite, since he actually *did* know what had been going on in this region, but his captors didn't have to know that.

Don Abraham looked a little surprised as he turned his hawk-like gaze toward Braddock. "What is your name, sir?"

"G.W. Braddock."

"And you claim you are merely passing through this ranch, señor Braddock?"

"It's not a claim, it's the truth. I'm on my way to Los Pinos."

The vaquero who had done most of the talking earlier said, "This is a lie, Don Abraham. This gringo had never heard of Los Pinos until we told him about it earlier."

"I didn't know the name of the place," Braddock said, "but I was on my way to the nearest town. That's what I told your men. But they jumped me, anyway."

"He fought," the young woman called Rosalita said as she pointed the quirt accusingly at Braddock. "Why would he do that if he is innocent?"

"Perhaps because he feared for his life?" Ordóñez said. His weathered features were still solemn, but his voice held a trace of amusement. "Or at least for his eyes, which it appeared you were about to cut out with that quirt of yours." The old man raised a gnarled hand and brushed it through the air in a gentle wave. "Release him."

Instantly, the vaqueros let go of Braddock and stepped back. Don Abraham Ordóñez might be an old man, but clearly, he still carried a lot of weight around here.

Ordóñez went on, "If you truly know nothing of the evil that has befallen those of us along the border, señor, then you have my apologies for how you have been treated."

Braddock moved his shoulders around to straighten his clothes and slapped some of the dust off his shirt. "I don't know how I can prove it to you, but I've told you the truth. I don't have anything to do with your problems." He added the little lie again. "Today's the first time I've heard about any trouble in these parts. Of course, I've been on the trail for a while. Haven't really heard much news lately."

That could mean several things, including the possibility that he might be on the dodge from the law. Braddock didn't elaborate. Let the old man draw his own conclusions.

Rosalita jutted her chin out defiantly and said, "No matter what else he has done, he should be whipped for the indignities he visited upon me and Javier. He dumped us both from our horses onto the ground!"

"If you and your brother attacked him unjustly, then perhaps you are fortunate he did not do worse."

Rosalita glared at her father but didn't say anything else.

The well-dressed young man she had called Javier, who evidently was her brother, had been helped to his feet by some of the vaqueros. He glowered darkly at Braddock, too, but didn't join the argument. Braddock took note of the young man's arrogant truculence and resentment and decided that he might do well to keep an eye out for him in the future. Javier Ordóñez had the look of a back-shooter.

"Return señor Braddock's hat and gun to him," Don Abraham ordered. One of the vaqueros picked up those items and handed them to Braddock. He checked the gun to make sure dirt hadn't fouled it, then slid it into leather. He batted the hat against his leg a couple of times to get the dust off it and then settled it onto his head.

Another vaquero brought the dun to Braddock and gave him the reins. Don Abraham said, "I will take you at your word, señor Braddock, and I apologize for the harsh treatment you received at the hands of my men." He flicked a glance toward Rosalita. "And the even harsher treatment you almost received at the hands of my daughter. I owe you a debt of honor, and since it is late in the day, in repayment of that debt, I invite you to my home for supper."

"Papa, no!" Rosalita exclaimed.

Don Abraham went on, "Then, if you wish to proceed to Los Pinos, some of my men will escort you there and guarantee you safe passage." He smiled. "This is not a trick to take you out and have you shot, I assure you. If I wished you dead, it would be exceedingly easy to accomplish, right here and now."

"I reckon I know that, so I'll take *you* at your word, Don Abraham," Braddock said. Spending some time with the old ranchero might give him more information that he could use. He added, "I'm grateful to you for your hospitality," and swung up into his saddle.

Ordóñez turned his horse and motioned for Braddock to ride with him. As Braddock moved the dun up, he saw Rosalita stomping off toward the big black gelding she'd been riding. She looked like a spoiled child who wanted to throw a tantrum . . . which Braddock supposed was a pretty good description of her.

She and her brother rode behind Braddock and Ordóñez, and as the group headed southeast, paralleling the course of the Rio Grande as Braddock had been doing for a week now, he felt Rosalita's gaze fastened on his back.

He didn't have to look around to see that her eyes were filled with hate. He could feel it, like a knife driving deep into his body.

5

THE HEADQUARTERS OF RANCHO DEL HALCON WERE impressive. The sprawling, two-story, slate-roofed, stucco hacienda dominated the scene, along with the adobe wall around it and the big wrought-iron gates at the opening. Braddock guessed that the house was built around a central courtyard, probably complete with garden and fountain. That was the Spanish style, and since this ranch had been granted to the Ordóñez family by the King of Spain two hundred years earlier, Braddock thought it was likely the original settlers would have wanted a place that reminded them of home.

The hacienda compound was hardly the extent of the headquarters, however. Surrounding it were a number of outbuildings: a long building Braddock took to be a bunkhouse for the vaqueros; several cottages where other, more privileged employees probably lived, perhaps with families; a blacksmith shop, a smokehouse, and a couple of storage buildings; a stable and coach house; and a magnificent barn with large, separated corrals to both sides and behind it. Braddock saw a garden patch, a pigpen, and a chicken coop as well, all of which would go to provide food for the people who lived and worked here.

The place had the look of a highly successful and lucrative operation. But then Braddock thought about everything that had happened recently. Don Abraham still had some stock on the ranch—Braddock had seen the cows grazing as the group of riders approached—but losing that trail herd must have really hurt, along with the bank robbery in Los Pinos. It was possible that Rancho del Halcon wasn't doing nearly as well as it appeared to be, which would help explain why everybody's nerves were on edge around here.

Of course, having men bushwhacked and killed would give folks the fantods, too.

Men opened the gates in the wall around the hacienda. Braddock, Don Abraham, Rosalita, and Javier rode through the opening while the vaqueros peeled off and headed for the stable, no doubt to put their horses away.

A couple of men in servant's livery came out of the house and were waiting to take the horses when Braddock and the others dismounted. They shot startled looks at him from the corners of their eyes, obviously puzzled to see a big gringo come riding in with the don and the don's son and daughter. But since Braddock was with Don Abraham, the man who took the dun's reins nodded deferentially and said, "We will see that your horse is well cared for, señor."

"Gracias," Braddock responded.

A heavy wooden door with iron straps on it stood open. Rosalita strode through it into the house, followed by her brother. Don Abraham shook his head and said to Braddock, "My apologies for the lack of manners on the part of my children, señor. They were brought up for the most part without a mother, my dear wife having passed away when Rosalita and Javier were quite young, but that is no excuse for treating a guest in such a rude fashion."

"It's all right, Don Abraham," Braddock said. "Considering how things could have turned out if you hadn't ridden up when you did, I don't have anything to complain about."

"Yes, that was fortunate . . . for you. I wonder if your coming to Rancho del Halcon will prove to be as fortunate for the rest of us."

"I don't mean to cause any trouble. I'll be riding on to Los Pinos soon."

"Yes, but you will still be in the area. Throw a rock in a pond, and the ripples sometimes will spread out all the way to the edges."

"You reckon I'm a rock and the border country is a pond?"

"You are, perhaps, as hard as a rock. This I can tell about you, señor." Don Abraham held out a hand toward the hacienda's entrance. "After you."

Braddock looked around while Don Abraham issued orders to some of the servants. The house was luxurious inside, just as Braddock expected. Opulently furnished with heavy chairs and sofas, wrought-iron lamp fixtures, and thick, intricately woven rugs on the gleaming hardwood floors. Paintings in elaborately carved frames hung on the walls. Those walls were very thick, which lent the air a refreshing coolness. The interior was shadowy but not gloomy. This was a place of wealth and comfort stretching back two centuries. Braddock could feel the antiquity of it wrapping around him like an old, soft blanket.

There was no sign of Rosalita or Javier. Braddock supposed they had gone to their living quarters. He didn't really expect them to join him and Don Abraham for supper, not with the hard feelings the two of them held toward him.

After they placed their hats on a marble-inlaid table, Don Abraham ushered him to a book-lined study with a desk and two comfortable chairs in it. "Are you a man who likes to read?" asked Don Abraham when he saw Braddock eyeing the shelves full of leather-bound volumes.

"I am when I have the opportunity . . . which hasn't been that often in my life," Braddock answered truthfully. Most of his adult years had been spent tracking down lawbreakers as a Texas Ranger. Nor was there an abundance of reading material available in Esperanza.

"Please, pick out one or two volumes to take with you when you leave," Ordóñez invited. "An intelligent man should be able to read when he feels the need for mental stimulation."

Braddock said, "I'm obliged to you for the offer, but even though I can speak and understand Spanish well enough to get along, I'm not sure how well I'd do reading it."

"There are books in English, too. I read it, as well as French and German."

"You're an educated man."

Don Abraham shrugged. "Self-educated, for the most part. Although when I was a young man, my father sent me to the university in Mexico City for a time. I prefer life here on the ranch. Cities are too big, too crowded."

"I'm fond of wide-open spaces myself."

"Most men who spend their days riding alone are,"

Don Abraham observed. He gestured toward a sideboard with a decanter and snifters on it. "Brandy?"

"Of course."

"I hope before you leave later, you'll join me in here again for another drink and perhaps a cigar. Or . . . perhaps you would prefer to spend the night and start for Los Pinos in the morning. That might be wise." Don Abraham cocked his head slightly to the side. "One never knows what might be encountered in the darkness."

Braddock didn't know if the old man meant anything by that or if it was just a general warning. A man *could* run into all sorts of trouble riding the range after dark.

"Your generosity and hospitality are much appreciated, Don Abraham," Braddock said as he took a snifter of brandy from the don. "I may just take you up on that invitation."

Ordóñez lifted his snifter. "To your health, señor."

"And to yours, sir."

A few minutes later, one of the servants came to the study to announce that supper was ready. "I apologize that the meal will be only a simple one," Don Abraham said as they strolled to the dining room. "We were not expecting company, of course."

"After a lot of meals of beans and bacon beside a lonely campfire, I'm sure it'll seem like a feast to me," Braddock assured him.

The dining room was just as elegant as the rest of the hacienda, with a table long enough for a dozen people. "Please, sit at my right hand," Don Abraham said as he gestured toward the chair.

Braddock did so. A glass of wine was waiting for him. The two places to Don Abraham's left were set for a meal, as well, and had glasses of wine next to the china and silver. For Rosalita and Javier, Braddock supposed, but he still didn't believe either of the siblings would join them.

He was wrong about that. A moment later, Rosalita Ordóñez swept into the room and came toward the table with elegant movements. Don Abraham got to his feet, and Braddock followed suit.

Rosalita was no longer dressed for riding. Her white shirt and black vest and trousers were gone, replaced by a dark blue gown with short, lace-decorated sleeves and a neckline that left her shoulders mostly bare and swooped to reveal the upper swells of her breasts. A necklace set with sparkling gems looped around her throat. Jeweled combs held back her raven hair.

She was breathtaking, thought Braddock, and it wasn't just because they were in this isolated border hacienda with no competition. She would have been just as beautiful in the finest dining rooms of Boston, London, or Paris, surrounded by the ladies of high society.

"My dear," Ordóñez murmured. "Will your brother be joining us, too?"

"You'll have to go find him and ask him yourself, Papa," Rosalita replied. "I am not Javier's keeper."

"Of course not."

Braddock said, "Señorita Ordóñez, you look lovely this evening."

"Gracias, señor Braddock. But do not mistake my presence for approval of my father's invitation to you. I still do not trust you."

"Rosalita!" Don Abraham exclaimed. "Such discourtesy to a guest in this house is unacceptable."

Braddock smiled and said, "That's all right, señorita. Trust has to be earned. But since I probably won't be around here long enough for that, I'll settle for you tolerating me."

She regarded him coolly. Her expression was unreadable, but at least he didn't see blatant hate in her eyes right now. He suspected that she was still a long way from warming up to him, though.

And as he had said, he wouldn't be around long enough for that.

Don Abraham held Rosalita's chair for her, then he and Braddock resumed their seats. Braddock looked across the table at her as she picked up her wine glass and sipped the dark red liquid.

"What is your line of work, señor Braddock?" she asked as she set the glass down.

"That is not a very polite question, Rosalita," her father said in a chiding voice.

Braddock still smiled. "That's all right, Don Abraham. I'm between jobs at the moment, señorita."

Strictly speaking, that was true. His true profession was hunting down owlhoots and lawbreakers, but he took on other work from time to time. John Edward Slattery hadn't offered to pay him anything, though, not even expenses, so right now, he didn't have an employer.

"I do not believe you will find work in Los Pinos."

"You never know."

The servants brought out the food then. Bowls of savory stew with chunks of what Braddock knew was goat meat floating in them, plus tortillas with beans, strips of seared beef, and peppers. As Don Abraham had said, nothing fancy, but very flavorful and filling. Braddock knew that because he had eaten the same dishes many times in Esperanza, sharing most of his meals with the mission priest, who was the closest thing he had to a friend in the world.

Braddock wasn't going to bring up the troubles that had plagued the Rancho del Halcon until he and Don Abraham returned to the don's study for brandy and cigars. He didn't figure rustling and bushwhacking were appropriate subjects for dinner conversation. But he had reckoned without Rosalita's bluntness.

"Between the theft of my father's cattle and the men shot from ambush, your countrymen have murdered almost a dozen of my father's vaqueros, señor Braddock. Surely you can understand why I do not care for the fact that you are under our roof this evening."

"As I've mentioned more than once, I didn't have anything to do with any of those crimes, señorita. Would you have all men punished for the sins of a few?"

The smile she gave him was icy. "If you are speaking about Texans, perhaps that would be a good course to follow. But first you would have to find some who have not sinned."

Braddock chuckled and said, "That would be a pretty tall order, all right. But not all of them have sinned against *your* people."

"Enough have," snapped Rosalita.

Don Abraham said, "The table is no place for arguments."

The gaze Rosalita directed across the table at Braddock was intent. He saw something he couldn't identify shifting around in her eyes. It might have been a trace of respect, but he couldn't be sure.

She said, "Perhaps when we have finished our meal, señor Braddock will walk with me in the garden and explain to me why I should not dislike him."

Don Abraham looked surprised. Braddock felt that way, but he was skilled at keeping his reactions from showing on his face. He sipped his wine and said, "That sounds very intriguing, señorita. I'd be happy to."

Ordóñez frowned and said, "One of the female servants will accompany you, of course."

"Of course, Papa. I meant nothing improper by my invitation to señor Braddock. But since he is here, he should have the opportunity to convince me that not all of his kind are in league with the Devil."

Don Abraham still didn't look happy about it, but he nodded, waved a hand at the food, and said, "Eat, both of you."

Since Rosalita had brought up the subject, Braddock said, "I'd like to hear more about the problems you've been having, Don Abraham."

Ordóñez told Braddock about the early morning raid that had netted the rustlers the trail herd and cost the lives of several vaqueros.

"From the sound of it, that was a gang from Texas, all right," Braddock agreed. "Or at least, they were pretending to be from Texas."

"My cattle are now on the other side of the river, that is all I know," Don Abraham said with a shrug. "I believe my man when he said the thieves looked and sounded like gringos. As for the ambushes, no one has ever seen the men who fired the fatal shots, so we know nothing about them, but it is reasonable to believe the same men are responsible."

Rosalita said, "You are a well-respected man, Papa. None of our people would set out to hurt you like this."

"Not many successful man achieve that success without making a few enemies along the way," Braddock said. "At least, that's what I've observed in the past."

Don Abraham smiled solemnly. "I have lived a long time. Most of the enemies I have made are no longer in this world. I cannot think of any who would set out to ruin me. The theft of the cattle was bad enough, but the robbery of the bank in Los Pinos and the deaths of my men since then . . ." He shook his head. "I hate to think what may happen to the Rancho del Halcon after all the many years it has been in my family."

"Nothing will happen to it," Rosalita said. "We will root out the vipers and crush them!" She stared at Braddock. "Wherever we may find them."

"You asked me to walk with you in the garden," Braddock reminded her.

"What better place for a viper to be lurking?" she replied coolly, without hesitation.

It was all Braddock could do not to laugh. Rosalita was single-minded in her determination not to trust him and to dislike him. It was almost as if she sensed her animosity toward him easing a bit and didn't want to allow that.

They finished the meal, drank the last of the wine in the bottle that sat on the table, and then Don Abraham said, "I will be in my study, señor Braddock. Please join me there when you have finished your stroll in the garden with my daughter."

"I'll do that, Don Abraham," Braddock said. This time he stood up and went around the table to hold Rosalita's chair for her as she came gracefully to her feet.

Don Abraham frowned at the place where Javier was to have dined, and the still full glass of wine next to it. "Your brother could have joined us," he said to Rosalita.

"His pride was wounded," she said. "He would rather nurse that grudge alone."

Braddock offered his arm to Rosalita. She hesitated, then linked her arm with his and led him out of the dining room. They went along a corridor and out through a door into a large courtyard. The house was built around it, as Braddock expected. The rooms on the second floor opened onto a balcony edged by a waist-high stone wall wide enough to have flower beds built into the top of it. At regular intervals, pillars rose from the wall to support the overhanging roof. Braddock was able to see all that in the soft yellow glow from lit lanterns hung in the trees that dotted the courtyard, along with shrubs and more flower beds. He heard the soft, liquid music of a fountain coming from the center of the courtyard.

With a beautiful woman on his arm, it might have been a very romantic setting . . . if not for the fact that the woman professed to hate him.

Still, she was here, he was here . . . There was no telling what might happen.

Probably not much, thought Braddock as he glanced over his shoulder and saw a heavyset servant woman who had followed them from the house. She stopped and clasped her hands in front of her, keeping her distance but still well within sight of Braddock and Rosalita.

He let her lead the way. They came to the fountain. The light wasn't as good here, but Braddock assumed the servant/chaperone could still see them. He didn't plan on doing anything improper, anyway, and he was pretty sure Rosalita didn't, either.

She surprised him, though, as she slid her arm free from his and turned so that she could face him squarely. Her head tilted back a little so she could gaze into his face. She said, "Señor Braddock, do you give me your word you have nothing to do with the devils who are trying to ruin my father?"

"I give you my word, señorita. I bore no ill will

toward your father to start with, and after the gracious hospitality he has displayed, I certainly don't."

"Then perhaps . . . you would consider helping him."

The suggestion deepened Braddock's surprise. "Help him do what?" he asked.

"I want you to find the men responsible for what has happened and put a stop to their evil. I know it is probably too late to recover any of the stolen cattle or the money taken from the bank in Los Pinos, but if the campaign of terror along the border continues, my father will be ruined. He will lose Rancho del Halcon. And the men who own the other ranchos along the river, my father's friends, they will face disaster, too."

Braddock frowned. "You want me to cross into Texas and go after those outlaws?"

"I saw how you fought against our vaqueros." Her chin lifted a little. "I do not have to like you to know that you are a formidable man."

"Not so formidable that I was able to stop them from making me helpless," Braddock pointed out. "As you should know, since you were about to take that quirt of yours after me." He lightly touched the scabbed-over cut on the back of his hand where she had slashed him.

He couldn't see her face well enough to read her emotions, but she sounded embarrassed as she said, "I apologize for my behavior. I was caught up in the heat of the moment."

"Meaning you're hot-blooded," he said with a trace of mockery in his voice.

"Do not, how do the gringos say, push your luck, señor. I assure you, my blood is not heated at the moment. In fact, it is quite cold."

He could hear that in her voice. Quickly, he turned over in his mind what she had said. He hadn't expected such an offer, by any means, but it was an intriguing one. Even though he had just met Don Abraham Ordóñez, he instinctively liked the old ranchero quite a bit. Whoever those hell-raising varmints were and whatever they were after, he didn't want to see Don Abraham lose the ranch that had been in his family for two hundred years.

He would be helping out Rosalita, too, and even though he didn't harbor any unrealistic expectations where she was concerned, it just flat-out never hurt to have a beautiful woman owing you a favor.

The problem was, the Texas Rangers, in the person of John Edward Slattery, were already investigating the situation on the other side of the border. The similarities of recent events along the border, the mirror image, so to speak, led Braddock to believe everything was connected. Of course, it was possible there could be two completely different gangs operating independently, one above the Rio Grande, one below it, but for now, anyway, he was going to consider that a more unlikely possibility.

No, his next stop was still Los Pinos, he decided, but after that . . . *quien sabe?* Who knew where the lawbreakers' trail might lead?

Braddock was about to tell Rosalita that he would do what he could, without getting too specific about what he was promising, when a faint movement caught his eye and he looked past her and up toward the balcony on the far side of the courtyard. He made out a shadowy form standing there, and just as instinct made alarm bells begin to clang in his mind, flame spurted from a gun muzzle up there on the balcony and a shot crashed in the night.

6

———

BRADDOCK WAS ALREADY MOVING, HIS MUSCLES REACTING instantly and powering him forward as a slug whipped past his ear. He wrapped his arms around Rosalita and drove her backwards off her feet. Another shot blasted. Masonry chips flew from the short wall around the fountain as a bullet slammed into it.

Rosalita let out a startled cry that was cut short as she and Braddock crashed to the ground between two shrubs. Still holding her tightly, he rolled toward the fountain. He thought that if he could get it between them and the bushwhacker, Rosalita might be safe.

She started squirming, as if she believed he was attacking her, rather than trying to save her life. "Settle down!" he hissed into her ear.

Evidently, that was the wrong thing to say, because she started fighting him even harder. He knew that if she got loose, she might jump up and try to get away from him, thereby putting herself right into the line of fire.

Regretfully, he did the only thing he could. Loosely balling his right hand into a fist, he clipped her on the chin with a short, sharp blow that left her momentarily stunned but otherwise unhurt. As she went limp, he finished his roll behind the fountain. He heard water splash as another bullet came from the balcony, searching for them.

Braddock's Colt was still in its holster when he reached for it this time. He palmed it out, waited for another shot from the would-be killer, and as soon as it rang out, he came up on his knees and fired twice at the balcony where he had seen the assassin a moment earlier. Instead of a muzzle flash stabbing back at him, he heard footsteps running along the balcony. Whoever was up there had met more resistance than he expected, and he didn't want to continue trading shots.

Even though he'd had only a brief look around the courtyard earlier, and that by dim light, Braddock had taken note of as many features as he could and committed them to memory. As an outlaw-hunter, he had gotten into that habit, and it had proven to be handy in the past.

Now he recalled that a staircase was located in the corner where the bushwhacker was headed. He didn't think the gunman wanted to descend into the courtyard, but he wondered if there might be an opening to the outside of the hacienda up there at the top of the stairs. Houses were designed like that sometimes, to allow more air to move through the courtyard.

That thought flashed through Braddock's mind in a split second. Rosalita moaned but didn't move, so he figured she would stay put in relative safety for a little while longer.

He sprang to his feet and raced toward the stairs at the corner of the courtyard.

He could still hear the rapid footsteps above him and

knew the gunman hadn't gotten away yet. Taking the stairs three at a time was dangerous in the dark like this, but Braddock's instincts guided him unerringly. He bounded to the top of the staircase in time to see a figure running along a narrow passage between two adjoining wings of the building, just as he had suspected might be there. The light from the moon and stars outside the hacienda was bright enough for the fleeing bushwhacker's silhouette to be visible.

Braddock triggered twice more but judging by the way the bushwhacker spun around and threw more lead at him, the shots missed. Braddock didn't know where the bullets went, only that he wasn't hit. He plunged after the fleeing man.

The passage ended in a railing. When the bushwhacker reached it, he vaulted onto it and then leaped outward into the night. Braddock fired again, but the way the figure dropped out of sight so swiftly, he figured he had missed.

Normally, he carried the Colt with only five rounds in it, instead of six, so the hammer could rest on an empty chamber. So, the gun was empty now, and he paused long enough to lean his back against the wall of the passage and fish more cartridges out of his pocket. He thumbed them into the cylinder. Since the hacienda had a wall that ran all the way around it, the bushwhacker probably hadn't gotten away completely yet but was still somewhere inside the compound.

Braddock ran to the railing but stayed to the side, against the wall, so he wouldn't provide a good target if the gunman was lurking just below. He ventured a glance out into the open area between the hacienda and the outer wall. There weren't many places to hide on this side of the house, other than a few clumps of cactus.

Braddock's eyes searched the shadows. He didn't spot any movement, and there were no unusual shapes lying on the ground. He had thought that such a reckless leap from the second floor might have resulted in the bushwhacker breaking a leg or some such when he landed, but evidently, that wasn't the case.

After a moment, knowing that he was taking a risk, he threw a leg over the railing and found a foothold on the narrow ledge just beyond it. He was about to swing his other leg over and make the drop to the ground himself when the man he was after stood up from behind some cactus and fired.

The bullet spanged off the railing only a couple of inches from Braddock's hand. He lost his grip and, unbalanced, toppled over the railing.

Lithely, Braddock twisted in mid-air so that he landed feet first, but he wasn't able to stay upright, sprawling forward on his belly instead. That fall probably saved his life, as the gunman sent two more shots screaming toward him. The bullets flew above Braddock and thudded into the hacienda's thick wall behind him.

Braddock heard a woman screaming somewhere and figured it was the servant who had been chaperoning him and Rosalita in the garden. A man started shouting questions.

Braddock snapped a shot at the bushwhacker, who darted aside. Braddock's bullet smashed a cactus and sprayed juice and pulp through the air, but that was all. The bushwhacker dashed toward the wall.

Braddock surged up and went after him. He felt a little shaken from the fall, but he didn't allow that to stop him. He holstered his gun. If he had a chance to capture the would-be assassin alive, he would take it. Whoever the man was, he might be forced into answering some questions. And those answers could shed some light on the lawlessness gripping the border country.

The wall was too tall for a man to leap up and grab hold of the top. Braddock didn't see how the bush-whacker hoped to get out by fleeing in that direction. But then the man reached the wall, jumped, caught hold of something, and hung there for a second.

The son of a bitch had a rope attached to something on the other side of the wall and dangling on this side, thought Braddock. He had planned to get out this way all along, after gunning down the visitor to Rancho del Halcon.

The bushwhacker braced a foot against the adobe wall and started trying to haul himself up. His move-ments were frantic. He seemed desperate to get away, but that near-panic just slowed him down. Braddock leaped and caught hold of the man around the waist.

They both fell awkwardly to the ground at the base of the wall. As they grappled and slugged at each other, Braddock finally got a halfway decent look at his opponent.

That didn't help identify the bushwhacker, because he had a black hood pulled over his head, completely concealing his features. Braddock remembered how the members of the gangs ravaging the border country wore masks—on both side of the Rio Grande. This gunman might belong to one of those gangs, if indeed there were two separate groups of bandits and not just one.

Braddock got in a couple of good punches, but he absorbed some punishment, too. His head was spinning. He kept fighting anyway. Now that he had his hands on one of the varmints, he didn't want to let go.

Then the bushwhacker managed to get his pistol out of its holster and struck a vicious blow with it. The barrel raked along the side of Braddock's head and caused his brain to whirl even more madly. The bushwhacker broke loose from him and shoved upright. Braddock expected to feel the crash of a bullet the next second, but he couldn't do anything about it. His muscles refused to respond to his commands.

Shots boomed, all right, but they didn't come from the bushwhacker's gun. Braddock heard shouting and rapid footsteps and knew that men were coming from the hacienda. The bushwhacker knew it, too. He holstered his gun and whirled back to the dangling rope. He leaped and caught it. The soles of his boots thudded against the adobe as he walked up the wall. Bullets struck around him as he fled, but he didn't slow down. He reached the top, rolled over it, and dropped out of sight.

The running footsteps pounded up to Braddock and stopped. He rolled onto his side, lifted his head, and groaned. Don Abraham Ordóñez said, "It is señor Braddock. Help him up, carefully!"

Strong hands took hold of Braddock and lifted him to his feet. He felt the warm trickle of blood down his face from the wound on the side of his head.

Don Abraham stood in front of him and asked, "Señor Braddock, how badly are you hurt?"

Braddock found his voice after a moment and said, "I reckon . . . I'll be all right. The hombre just . . . walloped me on the head . . . with his pistol."

"I have sent men to search for him, but I fear he may have gotten away already. If he had a horse waiting on the other side of the wall . . ."

"Likely he did," Braddock agreed. "I didn't hear any hoofbeats, but I was pretty groggy. Still am, to be honest."

He recognized the men who had helped him to his

feet as some of Don Abraham's vaqueros. The don told the men, "Help señor Braddock inside. He needs medical attention."

Braddock was feeling steadier now and thought he could have made it into the hacienda by himself, but he didn't refuse the help. They took him back to the dining room, where Rosalita was waiting, along with the servant woman who had been their chaperone in the garden.

Rosalita hurried toward Braddock. He expected her to fuss over him, since he was injured, or thank him for protecting her from that bushwhacker's bullets, but she didn't do either of those things.

Instead, she hauled off and slapped him.

"Rosalita!" Don Abraham exclaimed. "What in heaven's name are you doing?"

The slap had set Braddock's brain to spinning again. He might have fallen if the vaqueros hadn't been supporting him by his arms. He stiffened his back, forced a smile onto his face, and asked coolly, "Did I do something to offend you, señorita?"

"I will not be manhandled!" she said. "No matter what the reason. This gringo grabbed me and threw me to the ground, Papa."

"Only because somebody was shooting at you," Braddock pointed out.

"Oh?" She gave him a defiant stare. "And how do you know that the man was not shooting at *you?*"

Braddock frowned as he considered the question and realized that he couldn't answer it. As close as he and Rosalita had been standing to each other, as bad as the light in the garden had been, there was no way of being certain which of them had been the bushwhacker's target.

It was even possible that the varmint had wanted both of them dead.

"Whoever he was shooting at, I'm glad both of us are all right," Braddock said. "You weren't hurt, were you?"

"Only from when you threw me to the ground and hurled yourself on top of me. For taking such liberties, you are fortunate my father does not have you whipped and then force you to marry me."

"Please, Rosalita," Don Abraham said. "I'm sure señor Braddock meant no disrespect or insult to your honor. He was merely trying to keep both of you from being hurt."

Braddock nodded. "That's true."

Rosalita just sniffed and turned away. She left the room, but not without glancing back over her shoulder at Braddock. Once again, he found her expression impossible to read.

Don Abraham had Braddock sit down at the dining table. In response to his order, a female servant brought a basin of hot water and a clean cloth and swabbed the drying blood away from the wound on Braddock's head. Don Abraham leaned closer and studied it intently before saying, "I do not believe any stitches are required." He straightened and told another servant, "Bring tequila."

"That's a good idea," said Braddock. "I could use a drink."

Don Abraham smiled. "I'm not having it brought for drinking, although if you wish, we can certainly partake of it that way, too."

"You had more in mind using it to clean this place where I got clouted," Braddock guessed.

"It is a very good disinfectant."

Braddock laughed. "Good for man, inside and out."

A footstep made them both turn to look toward the dining room's entrance. Javier Ordóñez stood there, a puzzled look on his face and his dark hair tousled.

"I thought I heard shooting and shouting," the young man said, "but then I decided it must be a dream because I had been sleeping. Then I heard Rosalita slam the door to her room. What is going on here, Papa?"

"Nothing with which you need concern yourself," Ordóñez said. "Someone took a shot at señor Braddock and your sister while they were walking in the garden."

Javier scowled. "What was *he* doing, walking in the garden with Rosalita?"

Dryly, Braddock said, "That bothers you more than the fact that we were bushwhacked, does it?"

Javier flushed angrily. "Is Rosalita unharmed?"

"She is," Don Abraham answered solemnly. "And señor Braddock is injured but not seriously, apparently."

Javier snorted and turned away. He tried to stalk imperiously out of the dining room, but a slight hitch in his gait took away some from his haughty attitude.

"He's still a little banged up from that ruckus earlier today," commented Braddock when Javier had left the room. "I'm sorry, Don Abraham."

Ordóñez waved away the apology. "My son brought his troubles on himself, as he usually does. None of the blame is yours, señor."

The servant arrived with a bottle of tequila. She soaked a cloth with the fiery liquor, then held it to the wound on Braddock's scalp. His breath hissed between his teeth. It felt like somebody was pressing white-hot coals to his head, but the sensation passed quickly and the sharp pain subsided to a dull ache. The woman placed a pad of clean cloth over the wound and then bound it in place with a strip of fabric.

"That will serve as a bandage," Don Abraham said. "Now, you probably want some rest . . ."

"You wanted me to meet you in your study for brandy and cigars," Braddock reminded him.

"Yes, but after everything that has happened—"

"That doesn't matter. If there's something you want of me, something I can do for you, Don Abraham, I'd like to know what it is. I'd like to be able to repay you for your hospitality."

"And for the rudeness of my son and daughter?"

Braddock shrugged. "They're full-grown. I don't hold you responsible for them."

"Very well, señor Braddock," said Ordóñez, nodding slowly. "What I wished to discuss with you is a business proposition. I would like to hire you."

"I'm a decent hand, but probably not as good as the vaqueros you already have working for you."

"Not for ranch work, as I suspect you well know. I want to hire you, señor, to find those responsible for our troubles and put a stop to them."

Braddock didn't allow it to show on his face that, earlier in the evening, Rosalita had asked the same thing of him. She hadn't offered to hire him, though. In her case, it had been more like asking for a favor. Not surprising, since, like most beautiful young women, Rosalita probably was accustomed to getting whatever she asked for.

He asked, "What makes you think I could do a thing like that, Don Abraham?"

"You have the look of a capable man about you, señor. After tonight . . . your quick action to protect my daughter, your willingness to put yourself in danger to go after the intruder . . . I am more convinced of that than ever." Don Abraham put a hand on Braddock's shoulder. "Fate has brought you here, and I am a firm believer in fate. Will you help us, my friend?"

So now he was this rich ranchero's amigo, eh, thought Braddock. Well, as it happened, Don Abraham's goal and his own happened to line up, so Braddock didn't see any harm in playing along with the old man. He nodded and said, "I make no promises . . . except that I'll do what I can."

7

By morning, Braddock still had a slight headache from being pistol-whipped, but he had slept fairly well—probably aided by a couple of slugs of that tequila after his wound was cleaned and bandaged—and he almost had a spring in his step as he strode into the hacienda's dining room.

There was no sign of any of the Ordóñez family, but one of the servants was waiting for him. The same woman, in fact, who had followed him and Rosalita into the garden the night before.

"Buenos dias, señor Braddock," she greeted him. "Please have a seat, and I will bring your breakfast to you."

"With plenty of coffee?" asked Braddock.

The woman smiled at him. "Of course, señor."

A few minutes later, as she placed platters of tortillas, eggs, sausage, and peppers in front of him, Braddock asked, "Where is Don Abraham this morning?"

"Working on the range with the men, as he is accustomed to doing. Before he left, he said that when you arose, I was to give you this."

The woman delved in a pocket of the apron she wore and brought out a small canvas pouch. When she set it on the table next to Braddock's coffee cup, he heard coins jingle inside it.

"Don Abraham said you are now in the employ of Rancho del Halcon," the servant told him.

Braddock nodded. "In a manner of speaking." He picked up the bag and stuffed it in a pocket, knowing that Ordóñez intended for him to use it as expense money as he tried to track down the outlaws. That was what Braddock would do.

"What about señorita Rosalita and señor Javier?" he went on. "Where are they?"

The woman shook her head and rolled her eyes toward the second floor. "Neither have risen as of yet."

Braddock wasn't surprised. Don Abraham wasn't the sort who would demand either of them perform any duties around here, so they would be used to sleeping late. With no children of his own, Braddock was in no position to criticize anybody else for the way they raised their kids, but he couldn't help but believe it was a mistake to take it too easy on Rosalita and Javier. They would take advantage of it.

Braddock took his time with the meal, enjoying it, and when he was done, he lingered over a third cup of excellent, sweet but spicy coffee fragrant with the smell of cinnamon. In a way, he hated to leave Rancho del Halcon, but he had ridden down the Rio Grande Valley to do a job and it was still waiting for him.

He got his saddlebags and rifle from the bedroom he had been given and walked out to the barn. He found an elderly hostler inside. The man insisted on saddling

Braddock's dun for him. Knowing that the man probably had been a vaquero in his day and would still have his pride, Braddock didn't argue.

He did, however, check the cinches without letting the old-timer see what he was doing.

As he led the dun out of the barn, Braddock asked the hostler, "Los Pinos is straight on down the valley, right?"

"Sí, señor," the man replied. "Keep the Rio Bravo on your left hand, and you will not go astray."

"Muchas gracias, amigo." Braddock swung up into the saddle and rode out.

Nobody had taken any shots at him yet this morning, he mused. He thought the day was going pretty well so far.

———

NOBODY HAD EVER TOLD Braddock how far it was to Los Pinos. He'd been under the impression that it wasn't far from the ranch. As the hour grew closer to midday and he hadn't reached the town yet, he began to wonder if he had missed it somehow, despite what the elderly hostler had said about him not going astray.

Nor had anyone mentioned how large a settlement it was. But when Braddock finally came in sight of the buildings, he realized that Los Pinos was a good-sized town, with a business district that stretched for several blocks before ending at a large church. Residences sprawled around on several side streets.

Most of the buildings were adobe, but there were some frame structures built of lumber brought from the mountains to the south. Braddock even saw a few made of brick, including an impressive two-story building with a sign on it that read *BANCO*. That would be the bank that the masked bandits had robbed, he thought. As he rode past, he noticed a few pockmarks in the bricks and wondered if they came from bullets fired by the outlaws as they were getting away. Outlaws liked to throw lead around at a time like that. Tended to make the citizens keep their heads down and stay out of the way.

One of the adobe buildings up ahead caught his eye. Like the bank, it had two stories, the only other building of that size in Los Pinos. The sign on it read *EL PLACER*.

Pleasure, Braddock translated. Well, that was a simple and effective name for a cantina, gambling den, and brothel. From the size of the place, he suspected it was all three of those things. Pleasure in all its forms, for sale at the right price.

Braddock steered the dun in that direction. His gut told him it would be a good place to start.

As he rode, he was aware of the eyes following him. This close to the border, Texans and other gringos wouldn't be an uncommon sight in Los Pinos, but at the moment he didn't see any other of his countrymen on the street. Wagons were parked in front of many of the businesses, horses were tied at the hitch rails, and men and women walked here and there. A few kids walked along the street, followed by a barking dog. There were no boardwalks, but other than that it didn't look a lot different from settlements on the other side of the border.

Braddock tied the dun at the rail in front of El Placer. The building took up most of a block on the north side of the street. It had three entrances, each an arched opening with a gauzy curtain over it to help keep out flies. Braddock went to the closest entrance, which happened to be the one in the middle, pushed the curtain aside, and stepped into the cantina's large main room.

It was cooler inside, a welcome relief from the midday heat. The buzz of conversation in the room lagged slightly as heads swung toward Braddock for a second, but it picked right back up again when the customers didn't find him all that interesting.

That was all right with Braddock. He didn't want to attract a lot of attention at this point.

El Placer had two bars, a long one to Braddock's right and a smaller one against the left-hand wall. The left side of the room was also where the gambling went on. Braddock saw a number of poker and blackjack tables, a roulette wheel, and a faro layout. All of them had players, even in the middle of the day like this.

A small stage was located at the back of the room in the center, with some empty chairs on it. Braddock assumed that was where the musicians sat when a show was going on. That show probably would consist of several good-looking young girls dancing, flicking their skirts up, and flashing their legs.

Most of the customers were at the long bar to Braddock's right. Others sat at a handful of the tables scattered through the large room. In the far right corner, past the bar, stairs led up to a balcony that ran around three sides of the room. Braddock assumed that the doors opening off that balcony led to the rooms where the whores plied their trade. Nobody was going up or down the stairs at the moment. More than likely, all the señoritas were still asleep, although they would be waking up soon for another day of delivering what this establishment's name promised—pleasure.

Pleasure for the customers, anyway. For the girls, it would just be a way of making a living.

Although the cantina was busy, there were plenty of open places at the bar. Braddock eased into one of them. A stocky bartender in a dirty white shirt and a black vest came up on the other side of the hardwood, nodded, and said, "Señor?"

"Cerveza, por favor." It was still too early in the day for tequila.

The bartender drew a glass of beer and put it in front of Braddock. While riding from the ranch, Braddock had taken the coins out of the pouch Don Abraham had left for him and distributed some of them through his pockets while caching the others in his saddlebags. He took one of the silver pieces from his pocket and slid it across to the bartender, who deftly made it disappear.

Braddock picked up the glass and half-turned so he could look around the room while sipping the beer, which was both warm and watered-down. He wasn't the only gringo in here. A black-suited, pale gent dealt cards in one of the poker games. He had the look of a consumptive, and the rattling cough that came from him as he set the deck down confirmed that. Braddock saw other Americans here and there, all young and wearing range clothes. Probably cowhands who had come across the river from some of the spreads in Texas. Or it was possible they were on the dodge, having forded the Rio Grande because things had gotten too hot for them north of the river.

Someone bumped heavily into Braddock from behind. The beer in his glass sloshed but didn't spill. Braddock turned quickly. A collision like that was often a way of picking a fight. Maybe one of El Placer's other customers didn't like his looks or just felt proddy.

Instead, Braddock saw a slightly built young man with lank black hair falling in front of his face who ducked his head and cringed as if afraid that Braddock was going to strike him. He wore ragged clothes and clutched a broom.

"A . . . a thousand apologies, señor," he stammered. "I m-most humbly beg your pardon. Never in a hundred years would I have run into you in such a j-jarring fashion—"

"Take it easy," said Braddock, breaking into the frightened flood of words. "No harm done."

The bartender walked up and slapped a hand on the hardwood. The sharp crack made the young man jump and flinch.

"Chuco! Get away from that man. You're not even supposed to be in here right now. What do you mean, bothering the customers like that?"

"I . . . I am so sorry, señor Rodriguez, I meant no harm—"

The bartender sneered and said, "I know what you meant to do." He took the dirty towel that was draped over his left shoulder and snapped it like a whip at the young man, who dropped the broom, flung his arms up to protect his head, and cowered.

"It's all right," Braddock said, adding again, "No harm done—"

The bartender ignored him and yelled, "Get out of here, Chuco!"

Keeping his head down and his back hunched, the young man picked up his broom and hurried toward the nearest of the three exits, dragging his right leg behind him because evidently it was lame.

"I am sorry, señor," Rodriguez growled. "I pay that imbecile to sweep up, but sometimes he sneaks in to beg drinks or coins from the customers. He is fortunate I only chased him out and did not feel like beating him."

"You called him Chuco," said Braddock. "That means filthy, doesn't it?"

"Sí." Rodriguez laughed, revealing a gold tooth. "A good name for him, don't you think?"

Before Braddock could respond, he heard hoofbeats in the street outside, followed by a scream.

8

MOST OF THE PEOPLE IN THE CANTINA IGNORED THE commotion outside. A few men idly turned their heads toward the entrances as if they were curious . . . but not curious enough to stand up and walk over there to check.

Braddock was the only who started in that direction, after placing his half-empty beer glass on the bar.

"Señor, do not trouble yourself—" Rodriguez called after him, but Braddock ignored the bartender. Something about that scream had sounded familiar.

As he pushed aside the curtain over the arched opening and stepped out, he saw a cluster of half a dozen horses to his right. The dust hanging in the air told him the horses had swept up to the hitch rails and been reined in there. One rider was out a little in front of the others. His horse, a big gray stallion, reared up on its hind legs and neighed angrily as it pawed at the air with its steel-shod front hooves.

Cowering on the ground almost directly below those flashing hooves, in danger of being trampled by them, was the ragged young man called Chuco. He screamed again in terror.

The big man on the gray stallion just laughed. He could have brought the horse under control and backed off so that Chuco was no longer in danger, but he made no effort to do so.

Braddock, however, strode forward and reached up with his left hand to grasp the gray's headstall. He pulled the horse to the side while Chuco managed to get to his hands and knees and scramble the other direction, getting out of harm's way.

As the gray's front legs came back down on the ground, the rider cursed and pulled his left foot from the stirrup, which was ornately decorated with fringe and silver conchos like the rest of the saddle. He lashed out with a kick aimed at Braddock's chest.

"Get away from my horse, you gringo dog!" he yelled.

Braddock twisted aside so that the kick missed. He didn't think this man would be as easy to unhorse as Rosalita and Javier Ordóñez had been the previous day, so he didn't even try. He just moved back smoothly and dropped his right hand close to the butt of his Colt in case the rider or any of his friends made a play. They looked like the sort of men who might.

The big man finally brought his skittish mount under control. He threw his right leg over the saddle and dropped lithely to the ground instead of dismounting in the regular fashion. He crouched slightly and his hand drifted toward his gun, but he must have seen that Braddock was ready to match him, draw against draw, and thought better of it. Straightening, he growled, "You are a brave man, gringo . . . or a very foolish one."

"I just didn't want to see that poor fella get trampled to death," Braddock said.

"Him?" The man nodded toward Chuco and looked astounded, as if he couldn't believe that anyone would step up to defend such a worthless specimen of humanity. "Even if my horse had pounded him into the dust, no one would have ever missed him!"

"Whether a man would be missed or not, he still has a right to live."

"Oh, ho!" The booming laugh had no genuine humor in it. "You are a philosopher, eh, señor?"

Braddock grunted. "Not hardly."

Now that gunplay didn't seem quite so imminent, he took a better look at the man he was confronting, and those who had ridden into Los Pinos with him.

The man doing the talking was the biggest of the bunch, almost as tall as Braddock, with broad shoulders stretching a homespun shirt that once had been white. Time and dirt had dulled it to a light gray. He wore tight green trousers with embroidered decorations down the outside of the legs. His broad-brimmed sombrero was black. The clothes weren't cheap or ragged, just well-worn and covered with trail dust.

The black gunbelt around his waist and the holster attached to it were the most well-cared-for items he wore, along with his boots and the gun in the holster.

The men with him were dressed much the same. They didn't appear to be like working vaqueros, although they might have been.

That left two likely occupations for them: bandits or revolutionaries.

Of course, most of the time, those were the same thing.

"What are you doing in Los Pinos, eh?" the big man demanded.

Before Braddock could answer, the man noticed that

Chuco was trying to crawl away surreptitiously. He took a long step and aimed a kick at the ragged youngster's rump. Chuco sensed it coming, yelped in alarm, and jumped out of the way. He leaped up and hurried off down an alley, dragging his bad leg but moving pretty fast in spite of it. The big man and his friends thought that was hilarious.

Then the man sobered and turned back to Braddock. "I asked you what you are doing here."

"Are you the law in Los Pinos?" Braddock drawled, knowing full well that wasn't the case.

The question prompted more laughter from the big man's friends, but they shut up instantly when he glared at them.

"Not the law," the man said, "but I like to think the good citizens of this town are under my protection."

Which meant they were bandits who collected tribute to leave the businesses in the settlement alone and carry out their raids elsewhere. If that were the case, they might not be happy about somebody else coming along and robbing the bank.

Unless, Braddock mused, they had decided to put on masks and rob the bank anyway. That would be a nice trick, taking tribute to protect the town against thieves . . . and then raiding it themselves, anonymously.

He was getting ahead of himself, Braddock knew, but it was a theory worth keeping in mind for the time being, until he found out more. The big man was still glowering at him expectantly, so he said, "I'm just passing through, amigo. No hurry, and no real destination." He jerked his left thumb over his shoulder. "I was just inside having a drink. Maybe we can put this little fracas behind us, and you can join me."

The big man frowned, apparently thunderstruck by

71

Braddock's gall. "You lay hands on my horse," he said, "and then ask me to have a drink with you?"

"I just figured that on a hot day like this, the local undertaker would appreciate not having to pick up a dead body and do something with it. That's the only reason I stopped you from trampling that hombre."

One of the other men laughed and said, "The undertaker would not bother with the likes of Chuco. There is a pen full of hogs down the street. They would take care of him!"

The others chuckled and nodded.

The big man, evidently their leader, nodded and said to Braddock, "I don't like gringos, but there is something about you, amigo. Not many men would be bold enough to stand up to me, Valentín Bernal, the Lightning Bolt of Tamaulipas." He thumped a fist against his chest as he spoke his name. "So I will have that drink with you, and decide later whether or not to kill you, señor . . .?"

"Braddock," the Texan supplied. "G.W. Braddock."

By now, there wouldn't be many down here below the border who would remember that there once had been a Texas Ranger by that name.

Or so Braddock hoped.

ONCE THEY WERE INSIDE, Valentín Bernal led the way to a large table toward the back of the room. Several men were sitting at it, but as soon as they saw that Bernal was headed in their direction, they stood up and moved hastily to another table. Bernal and his men surrounded the one where the other men had been sitting and took their seats. Bernal waved Braddock into the empty chair on his right.

"The place of honor, señor," he said mockingly.

Braddock knew that wasn't it at all. Bernal just didn't want Braddock's gun hand right beside him. Braddock didn't hesitate, though. He sat down next to the big man.

Without being asked, Rodriguez, the bartender, brought over a couple of bottles of tequila. Bernal's men uncorked the bottles and began passing them around. Braddock swallowed a healthy slug when Bernal handed him the bottle after taking a drink.

When he had entered the saloon the first time, Braddock had thought it was too early in the day for hard liquor. Obviously, he was wrong. Bernal and his men guzzled down tequila like it was water.

"So, you are just passing through Los Pinos, you said?" Bernal said to Braddock.

"That's right."

"Gringos who pass through here, they are usually on the run from something."

Braddock shook his head. "I've never cottoned much to running. However . . . I do know the meaning of discretion and realize that sometimes the climate may be better for a man elsewhere."

Bernal guffawed and took another drink. "The climate on the other side of the Rio Bravo, sometimes it is even hotter than on this side, eh?"

"Can happen," Braddock replied with a shrug.

"Did you ride directly here from the border?"

"No," Braddock said. "As a matter of fact, I spent last night at a rancho northwest of here. Rancho del Halcon. Do you know it?"

A scowl darkened Bernal's face. "I know of it," he said. "Part of the old Ordóñez land grant. Don Abraham Ordóñez owns it. He has a very beautiful daughter. Or so I have heard."

Bernal didn't talk like a man who had only heard tales of Rosalita's beauty. He sounded more like someone who had witnessed it with his own eyes.

"She is beautiful," said Braddock, "but very full of herself and arrogant."

Bernal snorted and shrugged. "The right man would know how to make her more docile."

"I suppose he could try. He might even succeed . . . if she didn't cut his throat in his sleep."

That brought a grin to Bernal's rugged face. "Sí, he would have to be careful!" He changed the subject by asking, "Don Abraham, he is a friend of yours?"

"Not at all," Braddock said coolly. "I never met him before yesterday. I'm grateful to him for a night's hospitality, but that's all."

"You owe him no debt?"

"None big enough to speak of."

Bernal regarded Braddock shrewdly for a long moment, then said, "As I told you, I find something oddly likable about you, señor Braddock. I think perhaps we are much alike, you and me."

"Maybe." Not in a million years would Braddock want to be like this bandit, but he wasn't going to tell Bernal that.

"Instead of passing through Los Pinos, why don't you stay around for a while? It could be that something of interest to you might come up. A business opportunity, shall we say?"

"Even a man in no hurry, with no real destination, can't afford to pass up too many opportunities."

"Ay, this is true." Bernal jerked his head toward the bar. "Rodriguez rents some of the rooms upstairs. He'll even supply a girl to go with it."

Braddock thought about the hundreds, if not thousands, of sordid transactions that would have taken place on any bed in El Placer, and said, "I believe I'd rather find somewhere else to stay."

Bernal chuckled. "I cannot blame you for that, amigo. Try the hotel on the other side of the street, in the next block. I'm sure there will be a room for you there, especially if you tell them that you are the amigo of Valentín Bernal, the Lightning Bolt of Tamaulipas."

"Sounds good. I'm obliged to you."

"De nada," Bernal said with a wave of his hand. "If all goes as I hope, any obligation you feel toward me will soon be paid in full." He paused and shook his head. "Life is exceedingly strange, is it not?"

"I can't argue with that," replied Braddock, "but what makes you say it?"

"Half an hour ago, I was ready to kill you. To be honest, I am still shocked that I did not. And yet now, I believe that we will be great friends. Life can certainly change quickly, can it not?"

"It can."

"So have a care, my friend," Bernal said, "that it does not change back just as quickly . . . and fatally."

9

JUST AS BERNAL HAD SAID, THE CLERK AT THE HOTEL WAS more than happy to accommodate Braddock. Eager, in fact. The man bobbed his head and promised that even if the hotel had been full—which it was not—he would have moved heaven and earth to find a room for the distinguished visitor from north of the Rio Bravo.

Braddock suspected that most people in Los Pinos would not want to get on the bad side of Valentín Bernal, the Lightning Bolt of Tamaulipas.

The hotel was only a single story. Braddock carried his rifle and saddlebags along the hall to the room the clerk had given him. He had left the dun at a nearby livery stable, with promises of excellent care from the hostler. Braddock had mentioned Bernal's name there, too.

The hotel room actually looked pretty comfortable. The bed had a metal frame and a thick mattress with a colorful comforter on it. A woven rug was on the floor. An ornate crucifix and a portrait of the Madonna and Child hung on one wall, on either side of a mahogany wardrobe. Braddock looked at the painting and shrugged. He wasn't sure that what had brought him to Los Pinos could be described as the Lord's work, but he would try not to do anything too sinful while he was here . . . at least in this room.

More than likely he would have to break that commandment about killing before he was done, though.

It was early afternoon by now, and he hadn't had any lunch, only beer and tequila. He might have gone out in search of food, but the liquor and the heat that was building up inside the room took a toll on him. He decided to take a nap instead, sleep off the booze, then go out, find some supper, and prowl around the town later once the air had started to cool off. Bernal had told him that he would be in touch, so for now Braddock was supposed to just wait for the bandit to contact him.

Braddock set his hat on top of the wardrobe, unbuckled his gun belt and hung it on the ladderback chair he pulled close to the bed. He closed the curtains over the room's two windows, sat down on the bed and took his boots off, and stretched out.

He thought that sleep would come quickly, but it was stubbornly elusive. Valentín Bernal was a bandit; Braddock had no doubt of that. But was he the one behind the bank robbery, the rustling at Rancho del Halcon, and the raids on other ranches and towns up and down the Rio Grande valley? According to all the witnesses, the men responsible for those outrages had been gringos, but Braddock had been skeptical about that from the first. It was too easy to pretend to be something you weren't, and when all hell was breaking loose, eyewitnesses were easy to fool.

But if Bernal and his men weren't the ones Braddock

was looking for, that meant two gangs were operating in this area. Again, he couldn't rule that out, but he had no evidence supporting the theory, either.

He was turning all that over in his mind when he finally dozed off. He didn't fall into a deep sleep. Ingrained caution wouldn't let him do that in a situation such as this. Instead, it was a light slumber, with his senses still active on some level.

Because of that, he woke instantly when a faint noise came from the rear window. His eyes opened, but only the tiniest slit. Both windows were open a few inches to allow air to circulate in the room. Now the rear one was rising as someone outside lifted it slowly. That window overlooked an alley, Braddock recalled. Either somebody didn't know he was in here and figured on robbing the room . . .

Or somebody *did* know he was here and figured on killing him.

Braddock's thoughts went back to the previous night at Don Abraham's hacienda. Had the would-be assassin from the garden followed him to Los Pinos?

He kept his breathing deep and regular. He stood a better chance of getting answers if he allowed the lurker to continue thinking he was asleep. It seemed to take the man at least a quarter of an hour to raise the window high enough to slip through, although in reality it probably wasn't that long.

Finally, a leg snaked over the sill. A hand eased the curtain aside. With the light behind the intruder, he was just a silhouette to Braddock, who could tell that he wasn't wearing a sombrero and wasn't very big. That was all Braddock could make out, though.

Carefully, silently, the man climbed all the way into the room. The sluggish current of air brought the scent of unwashed flesh to Braddock's nostrils. That didn't mean anything. With most folks, it was more unusual for them *not* to smell dirty.

The thick planks of the floor didn't creak as the man moved across them. Braddock heard a very faint scuffing, as of bare feet on wood. Most likely a thief, he decided, who had decided to try and brazen it out anyway, even after seeing that Braddock was asleep on the bed. Little more than a phantom, the man headed for the wardrobe. Braddock had opened one of the doors and hung his saddlebags over it. That was what the thief had his eye on.

Braddock waited until the man had reached the saddlebags and stealthily taken them down from the wardrobe door before he sat up, pulled the Colt from the holster hanging easily within reach, and aimed it at the thief's back. The man jerked in alarm at the metallic ratcheting of the revolver's hammer as Braddock eared it back.

"Give me one good reason I don't blow a hole through you, amigo," Braddock said into the room's hot stillness.

The intruder's ragged clothes, slender frame, and tangled thatch of black hair gave Braddock a pretty good idea of his identity. That guess was confirmed when a familiar voice said in whining tones, "Please, señor, do not kill me. I mean you no harm, I swear."

"No, you don't want to hurt me. You just want to steal whatever I've got in my saddlebags."

The young man called Chuco looked back over his shoulder and ventured a feeble smile. "Making a living in a place like Los Pinos is very hard for one such as me, señor," he said. "Desperation makes men do things they would never do otherwise."

"Maybe so, but that defense won't stand up in court."

"There is no court in Los Pinos. There is only a constable, and he has a shrew of a wife, eight children, and a habit of consuming a jug of mescal every day before the sun reaches its zenith."

Braddock frowned. "You're an odd bird, Chuco."

Still smiling, the young man shrugged. "So I have been told, señor."

"What's your real name?"

"I . . . I do not recall. I have been called Chuco for so long—"

"All right, fine," Braddock interrupted him. "What am I going to do with you?"

"Forgive me for my foolishness and let me go?" Chuco suggested hopefully.

"I suppose it's that or kill you, since, like you said, there's no real law around here." Braddock paused. "I know what my friend, Valentín Bernal, the Lightning Bolt of Tamaulipas, would have me do."

Chuco's smile disappeared. "Please, señor," he said, "no matter what you decide to do with me, do not befriend that man. For your own sake. Bernal is evil. He and his men, many of whom are his cousins, have done terrible things. There is a good reason they are called the Bloody Bernals."

"He seemed friendly enough, once he got over being mad."

Chuco shook his head and said, "No, do not allow him to fool you. He is playing a trick on you, the, how do you say it, the double-cross. He hates gringos, all gringos."

"Seemed like he was thinking about asking me to join up with him."

"If he does that, it will only be so he can leave you for

the Rurales to catch the next time he does something illegal."

That actually made a kind of sense, thought Braddock. Meanwhile, since he had Chuco here and willing to talk, he might as well take advantage of that.

To put the shabby youngster a little more at ease, Braddock said, "Put those saddlebags back where you found them, and then I want to talk to you some more."

Chuco looked down at the saddlebags in his hand as if shocked to discover he was still holding them. Carefully, he draped the bags over the top of the open wardrobe door.

Braddock tilted the Colt's barrel up and eased the hammer down from its cocked position. He didn't holster the gun, though, but instead kept it casually ready.

"Tell me more about Bernal and his bunch," he said. "I want to know what I might be getting into."

"Nothing good, señor, of that I assure you. Bernal, he and his men are bandits. There is no way of knowing how many men they have killed or how many women they have defiled."

"On this side of the border, or do they cross over into Texas for their raids?"

Chuco frowned. Apparently, the question surprised him a little. He rubbed his chin for a moment as if thinking before he answered.

"Bernal preys on his own people. I have never heard of him crossing the border to commit his crimes. He probably fears the Rangers. They are devils. All Texans are. But on this side of the border . . ." Chuco spread his hands. "All he has to worry about are the Rurales, and so far he has eluded them with little trouble."

"That's no surprise," said Braddock. "The Rurales

only go after bandits when they don't want the competition."

Chuco sighed. "Sí, all too often, this is true."

"So Bernal's probably the one who robbed the bank here."

Chuco's eyes widened as he shook his head. "Ah, no, no, no. Bernal never raids along the border. He always goes farther south, to the bigger towns. Los Pinos is his, how do you say, his refuge. The place where he can come and rest and spend his ill-gotten loot. He would not befoul his own nest, as the saying goes."

That was interesting but not particularly helpful, thought Braddock. He'd had his eye on Bernal and his gang as the chief suspects in the lawlessness in this area. According to Chuco, that was unlikely, and Braddock didn't see any reason for the young man to lie about that. So he was left back where he'd started, with no real leads to the men he was after.

"Well, you sure make it sound like it would be foolish to get mixed up with Bernal," Braddock commented.

Chuco bobbed his head. "Very foolish, señor. Very foolish."

"If Bernal didn't hit the bank here and isn't responsible for the rustling hereabouts, who is?"

Spreading his hands, Chuco said, "How would I know, señor? I am only a poor cripple."

"And people talk around you, because they don't really see you. Am I right?"

Chuco shrugged. "I hear things, it is true. But from everything I have heard, the men behind those raids were gringos who crossed the river from Texas."

"What about the other direction? Anybody from this side going over to raid in Texas?"

A wary look came into Chuco's eyes. Braddock realized that he might have pushed too far. Despite his lowly circumstances, Chuco wasn't stupid. He said, "You ask many questions, señor."

"A man's always got to be on the lookout for something that'll be worth his time and trouble. I've heard rumors that somebody on this side of the river has been crossing into Texas to pull some jobs. I can't go back over there to stay, but I reckon I could . . . visit for a spell . . . if I had the right companions."

Chuco shook his head. "I cannot help you. I have told you everything I know. Now, please . . . either shoot me for trying to steal from you or let me go."

Braddock lifted the Colt. Chuco tensed. But Braddock just used the gun's barrel to gesture toward the raised window.

"Go on, get out of here," he said. "I don't feel like cleaning up a mess."

"Gracias, señor."

Chuco hobbled toward the window, his bad leg making his foot clomp on the floor. He pushed the curtain aside and started to climb out but paused halfway through, while he was perched on the sill.

"Please remember what I said, señor. Do not involve yourself with Bernal. There is too much of a chance it will end badly for you if you do."

"A man's got to do something with his time," Braddock replied with a shrug. "Taking chances keeps life interesting."

Chuco just shook his head solemnly, finished climbing out the window, and dropped out of sight. Braddock stood up from the bed, edge up beside the window, and leaned over to look out. He saw the ragged figure hurrying away along the alley with an awkward gait.

Judging by the light outside, it was late afternoon. Braddock didn't figure he would be going back to sleep, and besides, his stomach was telling him that it had been a long time since he'd eaten breakfast at Rancho del Halcon that morning. He went to the chair where his gun belt was hanging, slid the Colt into leather, and buckled the belt around his lean hips before he went to the small table where there was a basin of water and a cloth. He would wash up, and then see what an evening in Los Pinos held for him.

10

USUALLY, THERE WAS BETTER FOOD TO BE FOUND IN places other than saloons, so Braddock didn't head straight for El Placer when he left the hotel. Instead, he walked around the town until he found a small café where he was able to get a fried steak with a red sauce so hot that it made his eyes water, along with plenty of beans and tortillas. He washed the food down with strong coffee. Despite the long day, he felt pretty good as he left the café and strolled toward El Placer.

The sun was going down by now. Braddock kept an eye on the mouths of alleys where shadows had begun to gather. He hadn't forgotten about the attempt on his life the previous night. As far as he knew, nobody in Los Pinos had any reason to want him dead . . . but he had thought the same thing at Rancho del Halcon.

He pushed past the gauzy curtain over the entrance closest to the bar and found an open space. Rodriguez wasn't behind the bar this evening. Braddock supposed his shift was over. Instead, there were two men serving drinks, one of them small, middle-aged, and gray-haired, the other young, taller, and so gaunt he looked almost like a cadaver.

The gaunt bartender came over to Braddock to take his order. Braddock asked for beer and hoped it would be a little cooler than that he'd had earlier in the day. It wasn't. But it was wet, and he supposed it would do.

When he'd first stepped into the saloon, he had looked around but hadn't seen Valentín Bernal or anyone else he recognized. As he half-turned and leaned on the bar, he scanned the room again. Something drew his eyes to the roulette wheel, where several players stood with their backs to him, intently watching the spinning wheel and the bouncing ball. All the men wore sombreros except one. That lone man sported a black Stetson and wore a black vest over a red shirt. Judging by his outfit, at least, he was an American.

The ball finally settled into one of the spaces on the roulette wheel. All the players must have lost because a chorus of disappointed groans went up. The man Braddock had noticed reacted like the others, but as he tipped his head back to express his disgust verbally, he turned his body enough that Braddock was able to see his profile. Definitely a white man, although his face was deeply tanned. The hair under the black Stetson was crisp and fair.

Braddock had been about to take a sip of beer, but he stiffened and lowered his glass as he looked at the gringo at the roulette wheel. The man's name was Ed Montayne, and his name was in the book—the Doomsday Book, the Ranger Bible, the listing and description of all the known outlaws the Rangers were looking for, along with their crimes.

Ed Montayne was wanted not just in Texas, but in other states and territories, as well. He had a couple of murders hanging over his head, along with numerous charges for bank robberies, train hold-ups, horse theft, arson, and no telling what else by now. He had been well-known as a fugitive from the law while Braddock was still wearing a Ranger's star. Clearly, he had continued to elude capture during the past few years.

Well, there was nothing unusual about a man on the dodge in the States being in Mexico, Braddock told himself. Technically, *he* was an outlaw, and he was down here below the border.

He watched as Montayne placed another bet on the roulette wheel. Montayne lost again and, shaking his head, turned away from the wheel. He looked like he'd had enough, at least for now. He headed for one of the few empty tables, and along the way, he slipped an arm around the waist of a young woman who had been delivering drinks from the bar.

That was one big difference in El Placer between now and when Braddock had been in here earlier in the day. A number of women were circulating through the big room, all of them dressed in colorful skirts and blouses that left their shoulders bare and exposed most of their bosom. As Montayne steered the woman he had picked toward the table, she laughed and clutched at her neckline with her free hand to keep her ample breasts from popping out.

Montayne sat the woman down at the table and said in English, "You're gonna drink with me for a while, honey, and then we'll go upstairs." He signaled to the nondescript bartender for a bottle. The man put it on a tray and handed it to another of the serving girls.

"Something wrong with the beer, señor?"

The question came from behind Braddock. He glanced around to see the cadaverous bartender standing there. Braddock realized he had been holding the glass for several moments without drinking while he watched Ed Montayne. He shook his head, said, "No, it's fine," and took another sip of the warm stuff. He kept his gaze pointed away from Montayne for now. He didn't want the man to notice he was being stared at.

As far as Braddock could recall, he and the Texas outlaw had never crossed trails before. He had seen Montayne's picture on enough wanted posters that he was certain of the man's identity. But it was unlikely Montayne would recognize *him*. The only way that was possible was if someone had pointed Braddock out sometime in the past, when Braddock wasn't aware of Montayne's presence.

Still, he didn't want to alert Montayne to his interest. Montayne might not have anything to do with the trouble that had brought Braddock here, but he had a reputation as a bank robber and rustler. There was at least a chance he was mixed up in the fresh hell going on along the border.

Montayne drank and flirted with the girl he had claimed while Braddock finished his first beer and nursed another one. Braddock kept one eye on Montayne and the other on the entrances, watching for Valentín Bernal. The bandit hadn't put in an appearance when another man came into El Placer, looked around, and then headed for Montayne's table.

The newcomer was dressed like a vaquero. Braddock didn't recognize him. At the table, the girl was leaning on Montayne and giving him a good view down the valley her low-necked blouse revealed. She tipped her head back to show off the clean line of her throat and laughed at something the Texan had said.

That was when Montayne spotted the man

approaching the table. He must have recognized the newcomer, because he abruptly pushed the girl away and straightened in his chair, abandoning the casual slouch he had adopted. The girl pouted, but Montayne paid no attention to her now.

Braddock wondered briefly if the newcomer held some sort of grudge against Montayne. Gunplay might be about to erupt. But when the vaquero reached the table, he merely leaned down and spoke to Montayne, much too quietly for Braddock to make out any of the words against the hubbub of the room.

Montayne nodded curtly. The vaquero straightened and moved away from the table. The girl leaned toward Montayne and spoke in what Braddock figured were wheedling tones, judging by the expression on her face. She looked like she realized that something she wanted was slipping out of her hands, and there was nothing she could do about it.

Montayne talked to her for a couple of minutes, then reached inside a vest pocket and pulled out a coin. Braddock thought it was a five-dollar gold piece. The girl brightened up at that, but she still made a little face of disappointment as Montayne pushed the coin over to her. Five bucks was very good pay for a soiled dove, but maybe she had hoped to make even more if she got Montayne upstairs.

That wasn't destined to happen, at least right now. Montayne gave her a kiss, fondled her one last time, and then got to his feet. His hat was pushed back on his fair hair, but he tugged it forward and down as he turned toward the entrances. He walked out the middle one without looking back.

Braddock had only a couple of swallows left in his second beer. He drained them and set the empty glass on the bar, then sauntered toward the left-hand entrance, the one closest to him. That vaquero, if he really was a vaquero, had delivered a message of some sort to Ed Montayne. It must have been a summons, and the outlaw was on his way to answer it now.

Braddock wanted to catch a glimpse of whoever Montayne was meeting, if he could.

He stepped out into the warm night and moved quickly to the side so he'd be out of the light spilling through the entrance. Standing in the shadows, he looked along the street and spotted Montayne's tall shape walking away from him in the direction of the bank. A wild thought sprang to life in Braddock's brain. The raiders had hit the bank once already. Could they be targeting it again, even though there hadn't been time for the establishment to recover much?

Braddock's long legs carried him across the street at an angle. Even though he didn't appear to be hurrying, he covered the ground quickly enough that he drew even with Montayne on the other side of the street. Most of the businesses were closed for the night, so he didn't have much trouble sticking to the darker areas as he matched Montayne's pace.

Montayne wasn't heading for the bank. His destination turned out to be the livery stable, the same one where Braddock had left his dun. No light burned in there now, but one of the big double doors stood partially open. Montayne turned and slipped through the gap, vanishing into the darkness within.

Braddock stopped where he was and frowned as he peered across the street. Montayne had to have a good reason for going into the stable. Braddock wanted to know what it was. Making up his mind, he continued a short distance along the street, then turned and walked unhurriedly toward the other side with his head down. If anyone was watching from the stable, he'd just appear to be a man going about his business.

No shots rang out. No one challenged him. Braddock reached the far side of the street, stayed close to the buildings, and worked his way back toward the stable. Before he reached the doors, he stopped and pressed his back to the wall as he listened intently.

The murmur of men's voices came from inside. Braddock couldn't make out any of the words. He heard a faint rasping sound. A tiny, flickering glow sprang to life inside the barn. One of the men had struck a match.

Braddock had to get a look in there. He eased along the closed door toward the gap where the other one was pulled forward a couple of feet. He took off his hat and held it in his left hand as he edged an eye past the barrier and peered inside the barn.

Two men stood in the broad center aisle, toward the rear. One stood with his back toward Braddock, who was unable to see his face. Judging by the Stetson he wore, he was an American, too.

Ed Montayne faced toward the doors, but his attention was focused on the man he was talking to, so Braddock hoped the outlaw wouldn't notice that this rendezvous had an observer. A lantern hung on one of the posts that held up the hayloft. A flame burned in it but was turned very low, so it cast only a small circle of light that barely enclosed Montayne and the other man. The rest of the barn's interior was cloaked in deep darkness.

Braddock knew the rasp he had heard had been Montayne striking the match he'd used to light the lantern. Montayne had a wary look on his face. The other man was doing most of the talking, possibly trying to convince Montayne of something. Montayne wasn't going to be won over easily, though.

Braddock wished he could hear what they were saying. His eyes narrowed as he spotted a man-sized single door at the back of the barn, much smaller than the double doors in front where horses, wagons, and buggies could go in and out. That door was fairly close to where Montayne and the other man were standing, Braddock realized. If he could slip around there and open it a little without them noticing, he ought to be able to hear what they were talking about.

It was worth a try, he decided. He stole away from the gap between the front doors and put his hat on again as he circled the building.

It was pitch black in the alley alongside the livery stable, so Braddock had to be careful. If he ran into anything or knocked something over, it might alert the men inside. An owlhoot like Montayne would be skittish to start with. If he even thought anything might be wrong, he would bolt.

Braddock reached the back of the livery stable and catfooted along the wall toward the small door. If it was locked, this effort would be for nothing, but most folks never locked any doors. When he reached it, he wrapped his hand around the brass knob and carefully tried to turn it.

The knob turned. The catch clicked, too soft to be heard more than a foot away. Braddock maintained his cautious grasp on the knob with his right hand and once again took his hat off with the left, so the brim wouldn't get in the way as he leaned close to the door. He eased it toward him.

There were the voices, louder now. He heard Ed Montayne say, "—in on the plan."

Keep talking, thought Braddock. He wanted to be let in on the plan, too.

A light touch brushed against his cheek and then another against the top of his head. Something was falling on him. He jerked his head back and looked up, saw several more tiny bits of hay swirling down toward his face. There was another door up there above him, a hatch-like opening where bales of hay could be lifted from wagons with a block and tackle and swung inside to be stored in the hayloft.

Braddock's brain had barely registered that fact when a dark shape leaped from the opening and plunged down at him.

11

A STRAY BEAM OF STARLIGHT GLITTERED FOR A SPLIT-second on the blade of the knife clutched in the attacker's hand. Braddock twisted aside and threw his left arm up. That hand still held his hat. His forearm struck the man's arm and knocked it aside, causing the knife to narrowly miss him.

An instant later, the man's weight crashed into Braddock's head, shoulders, and upper chest, driving him off his feet to the ground. He dropped the hat.

The impact knocked the wind out of him and Braddock had to gasp for breath, but he didn't let that stop him from fighting. He groped out with his right hand and closed it on the collar of the man lying on top of him, pinning him down. At the same time, he tried to find the wrist of his attacker's knife hand before the man had time to plunge the blade into him. His fingers brushed against a sleeve. He clutched desperately and locked his fingers around the man's arm.

Braddock bucked up from the ground and heaved. He rolled and was able to throw the man off of him. The attacker grunted as he hit the ground. Braddock still had hold of his collar and his right wrist.

The man's left arm was free, though. He used that arm to launch a punch that slammed into Braddock's jaw. It was so dark back here behind the livery stable that some luck had to be involved in landing that blow. The man couldn't have aimed it that well. Luck or not, the punch drove Braddock's head to the side and made the world spin crazily around him for a second.

The small door in the stable's back wall slammed open. Braddock caught a glimpse of Ed Montayne charging out, the lantern in his upraised left hand, a Colt in his right. Montayne must have heard the commotion behind the building while he was having his meeting inside.

"Kill him!" a muffled voice cried.

The order came from the man who had leaped from the loft and tried to knife Braddock. Montayne had to be confused about what was going on out here, but there was only one other man out here besides the one who'd given the command, so he swung his Colt toward Braddock and pulled the trigger.

Braddock threw himself aside just as flame gushed from the muzzle of Montayne's gun. The bullet sizzled past his ear. His whirling brain was starting to settle down, the cobwebs from the punch cleared away by the danger in which he found himself. He clawed out his own Colt, tipped it up, and fired at Montayne.

The Texas outlaw ducked back through the door as Braddock's slug whipped past him and chewed splinters from the jamb. Through the echoes of the shots, Braddock heard Montayne yell, "You double-crossing son of a bitch!" Guns crashed inside the livery stable.

Knowing it was better to keep moving, Braddock

rolled again and came up on one knee. Montayne was out of reach for the moment, but the man who had tried to knife him was still back here.

Or was he? Braddock heard what seemed to be several sets of running footsteps. The same muffled voice he had heard a few moments earlier called, "Back here! Back here! Kill that man!"

Braddock bit back a curse. The knife-wielder was fleeing, but he had allies close by, allies he had just set on Braddock. Shapes loomed in the darkness as men charged toward him. Crimson flowers of muzzle flame bloomed. Bullets streaked out of the night and kicked up dirt around Braddock as he scrambled desperately toward the still open door in the livery stable's rear wall. Montayne might be waiting for him in there, but there was no cover for him out here.

Lead thudded into the stable wall. Braddock darted to one side and took cover in an empty stall. He crouched and waited, his eyes on the rear door.

Montayne appeared to be gone. The outlaw had dropped the lantern on his way out the front. Miraculously, it hadn't shattered. It lay on its side with the wick still burning, casting its feeble light across the hard-packed dirt aisle between the rows of stalls. At the edge of that glow, a figure sprawled face-down. Braddock remembered the shots and Montayne's shouted accusation about a double-cross.

Whoever Montayne had been meeting with, he had gunned the man down before fleeing the barn.

Braddock was curious about that man's identity, but discovering it would have to wait. The guns outside had fallen silent, but that didn't mean the men who'd tried to kill him were gone. No, he thought, they were still out there, trying to figure out their next move.

He knew what that move would be if he were in their position. He would send men around to the front of the livery stable to keep their quarry from escaping that way, then launch an attack from both sides.

Either that, or they could try burning him out. The stable's adobe walls wouldn't burn, but all that hay up in the loft and spread around in the stalls down here sure would. It would create enough of a blaze that blistering heat and choking smoke would drive him from his shelter.

With a fire, though, there was always the risk of it spreading. Braddock didn't think they would take that chance when they had him outnumbered and already pinned down.

Sure enough, men burst through the back door, shooting as they came. Coolly, Braddock returned their fire, triggering his Colt over the stall's side wall. In the glare from the muzzle flashes, he saw that his attackers wore long coats, pulled down Stetsons, and masks over the lower halves of their faces.

The outlaws he had ridden down here to find were right in front of him. Unfortunately, he was in no position to take advantage of that. There were too many of them. He spaced his shots and aimed carefully, saw two men stumble as his bullets found them, but in a matter of seconds he would be overrun.

It got worse. A shot came from the front of the barn and smashed into the side of the stall. More outlaws were charging in the front now, he saw from the corner of his eye. They had him in a crossfire, just as he'd expected.

Shots blasted from a darkened corner of the barn. Tongues of muzzle flame lashed out. The sharp cracks of the reports contrasted with the duller booms of handguns and told Braddock that somebody with a rifle was taking a hand in the fight. Those rounds lanced into the men attacking from the front and spun a pair of them off their feet. Taken by surprise, the other outlaws yelled in alarm and fell back, dragging their wounded with them.

Braddock triggered the final two shots in his Colt at the men in the back of the barn, who were retreating as well. Braddock and his unknown ally had fought off the attack—for now.

As he thumbed fresh cartridges into the revolver's cylinder, Braddock looked toward that front corner where the unexpected help had come from, but his eyes couldn't penetrate the thick shadows there. The only thing he could figure out was that the old hostler had been hidden somewhere in the stable when the shooting broke out and had decided to back his play. He called, "Much obliged to you, amigo, but we're still in a pretty bad fix here. If you can slip out, maybe you'd better do it while you've got the chance."

The only reply was the clack of a Winchester's loading lever as the man jacked another round into the rifle's firing chamber.

Braddock let out a grim chuckle and said, "Have it your own way, then. Better get ready—"

He didn't finish the sentence, because at that moment, a masked man leaped through the open back door with a burning torch in his hand. He threw it, spinning, toward the hayloft.

Braddock and the unknown man with the rifle fired at the same time, the blasts blending together. Both slugs smashed into the chest of the man who had just thrown the torch and flung him backward so he landed half in and half out of the door.

That deadly response wasn't in time to stop him from accomplishing his objective, however. The burning brand sailed into the hayloft. Within seconds, Braddock heard flames crackling and smelled smoke. They were going to risk a fire after all.

About half the stalls in here had horses in them. The animals were already spooked by the gun battle and had been stomping around and lunging heavily into the side walls. Now as they caught whiffs of smoke, they panicked and screamed and began kicking against the enclosures. Braddock's dun was among them, and he was damned if he was going to let his trail partner burn to death or be overcome by smoke.

"Cover me if you can!" he shouted to the man with the rifle. He jammed the Colt back in its holster and leaped out into the open.

Instantly, shots flared from the outlaws at the front and rear of the barn. Braddock felt a bullet pluck at his sleeve, and he would have sworn he could sense the warmth of another as it passed within a fraction of an inch of his cheek. Behind him, the Winchester cracked again and again, the blasts coming so fast they sounded like one long, rumbling roar of gun-thunder.

Braddock reached the nearest stall where a horse was lodged and slapped up the latch on the gate. He didn't have to open it. The horse smashed against the gate and threw it wide. The animal's big body shielded him to a certain extent as he ran to the next stall and opened it, as well. The result was the same: a frantic, stampeding horse.

Moving as fast as possible, Braddock freed the rest of the horses, including his dun. The air was thick with dust now from the pounding hooves, and that helped conceal Braddock's movements, too. The Winchester cracked a couple more times, then fill silent. Braddock ducked behind one of the gates he had just opened and drew the Colt again, ready to fight back if the attack resumed.

Except for the echoes, the shooting seemed to be done, though. The fire was burning fiercely in the loft, adding its smoke to the pall of dust in the air. The outlaws must have realized they weren't going to be able to get him without coming in here, and they didn't want to attempt that again. They might be lurking outside, though, waiting to get another shot at him.

Didn't matter if they were, Braddock told himself. He couldn't stay in here. The hellish glare from the flames was bright enough for him to see, finally, into the corner where his unknown ally had been. The spot was empty now. The rifleman had fled, and it was time for Braddock to do the same.

The man Montayne had shot was still lying face-down in the center of the aisle. It didn't appear that any of the horses had trampled him as they stampeded out. Braddock had figured the man was dead, but now, suddenly, he stirred slightly. Braddock spotted the movement through a gap in the swirling smoke.

Braddock couldn't leave the wounded man in here. He pouched his iron and ran through the smoke and dust until he reached the man's side. He bent down, hooked his hands under the man's arms, and dragged him toward the front entrance, which was closer. The man was solidly built and weighed quite a bit, but Braddock, grunting from the effort, kept moving.

They cleared the door. Braddock hauled the man several more feet before letting him slump face-down again. Braddock dropped to a knee beside the man and drew his gun. He twisted his head back and forth, searching for any signs of danger.

A number of the townspeople stood not far away, drawn by the gunshots and the fire in the stable. They stared open-mouthed at the flames, but nobody made any effort to put out the blaze.

Then Braddock heard a bell ringing. The crowd parted. Los Pinos had a fire wagon, it seemed. The vehicle, drawn by a couple of mules, rocked and jolted along the street from wherever it was kept. It came to a stop near the stable's open doors. Men crowded around it, some of them unrolling a long canvas hose attached to the big wooden tank on the back of the wagon, while others got ready to work the pump that powered the stream of water from the hose.

Braddock continued looking around warily, not convinced yet that he was out of danger, but it began to seem that way. He wouldn't put anything past that gang of masked raiders, but it wasn't likely they would make another try for him with this many people around. As the townsmen stretched the hose into the barn and got water spewing from it, Braddock finally holstered his gun.

A groan from the man he had dragged out of the stable made Braddock turn his attention to him again. He took hold of the man's shoulders and carefully rolled him onto his back so he could see how badly the hombre was hurt.

From the looks of the blood soaking the man's shirt and the two bullet holes in it on the left side of the chest, the man was done for, even though death hadn't quite caught up to him yet. However, that grisly sight wasn't what made Braddock stiffen in shock.

He reacted that way because the light from the blaze

inside the stable spilled into the street and clearly revealed the pain-drawn features of Texas Ranger John Edward Slattery.

12

BRADDOCK'S THOUGHTS WHIRLED FASTER THAN A TEXAS twister. He leaned over and said, "Slattery! Slattery, can you hear me?" He made his voice loud and urgent enough that he hoped it would penetrate all the commotion and register on Slattery's stunned brain.

The Ranger's eyelids fluttered. He let out a ragged sigh. For a second, Braddock thought that was the finish, that Slattery was gone, but then the man's eyes opened again. They didn't seem able to focus on anything.

"Slattery!" Braddock said again. "John Edward! It's me, Braddock. G.W. Braddock."

Slattery's head moved slightly. He seemed to be searching through the shadows that had to be gathering around him. "B-Braddock . . .?" he rasped.

"I'm here, John Edward." Braddock glanced around. With the blaze going on in the livery stable, nobody was paying any attention to them. No one was close enough to overhear anything they said. "What are you doing here? Who were you after?"

"D-Devil," Slattery choked out. Braddock didn't

know if he was referring to Satan or just calling somebody a devil.

"Are you talking about Montayne? Ed Montayne?"

A shudder went through Slattery, and again, Braddock thought he was dead. Slattery wasn't quite done for yet, though. He gasped, "Go to . . . Devil . . ."

Slattery was telling him to go to the Devil at a time like this? That seemed loco to Braddock. Maybe Slattery didn't actually know who he was.

"G.W." That whisper made it clear Slattery *did* know who he was, thought Braddock. But he still didn't understand that the man was trying to communicate to him. "Whole . . ."

The whole *what?* What was Slattery trying to tell him? Or was he talking about a hole in something? Or maybe even trying to say *holy.* He'd been talking about devils, after all, so mentioning something holy was at least related.

"Devil . . . Devil . . . Devil . . ."

This time the sigh that gusted out of Slattery's lips ended in a grotesque rattle. No mistaking it. The Ranger was dead. And he'd died without telling Braddock why he was in Los Pinos and what he'd been talking about with Ed Montayne. Montayne might not have known that Slattery was a Texas Ranger, but Slattery had to have been aware that Montayne was an outlaw, just as Braddock had been as soon as he laid eyes on the man. Slattery knew the Doomsday Book as well as Braddock did. Probably better.

However, it was a mystery that might not ever be solved, because Slattery was gone. His eyes stared sightlessly up at the night sky, which was dotted with swirling embers rising from the fire in the stable. Braddock rested his fingertips on Slattery's eyelids and gently closed them.

He stood up and looked around. Some of the bystanders had noticed them and were gazing curiously at the dead man. Braddock spotted the hostler he had dealt with earlier among them. He motioned to the man, who shuffled over and removed his sombrero.

"Yes, señor?" he said. "Is there something you require of me? I am sorry if your horse, he was lost in the fire—"

"I got all the horses out," Braddock interrupted him. "You may have quite a chore rounding them up, though. What I want to know is, was that you in there a few minutes ago with a Winchester, helping me out?"

He could tell from the confused look the man gave him what the answer was going to be. "Señor, I . . . I know nothing about that. I was at my home when a friend brought word that the stable was on fire."

"You don't sleep in there?"

"No, señor. Very rarely, and not tonight. My wife, she likes for me to be at home."

Braddock wasn't interested in the man's domestic arrangements. His instincts told him the hostler was speaking the truth. It hadn't been him who helped Braddock fight off the outlaws.

Then who could his mysterious ally have been?

For that matter, who was the man in the loft, the one who had jumped on him and tried to knife him? Braddock's mind flashed back to the previous night and the bushwhack attempt in the garden of Don Abraham Ordóñez's hacienda. That ambusher had fled as soon as it became apparent that his attack had failed. The man tonight had done the same. He was no coward; the leap from the hayloft door proved that. But neither was he the sort to stay and fight if he didn't win right away. It could have been the same man, Braddock decided. Someone could have followed him here from Rancho del Halcon. Anyway, it was common knowledge to those on the ranch that he'd been headed for Los Pinos.

The way the man had shouted orders as he fled told Braddock that he was accustomed to command, too. Could he have been that close to the mastermind behind the border troubles? Could he have had the man he was after right in his hands? Ed Montayne wasn't the boss; he had never been the sort to run things. But he would make a good segundo for whoever was in charge.

It was all too much to sort out tonight, Braddock told himself. He shook himself out of his momentary reverie as the hostler asked, "Was there anything else, señor?"

"I reckon not." Braddock dug in his pocket and brought out a double eagle. He pressed the twenty-dollar gold piece in the man's hand and said, "That'll help with the damages. What happened wasn't my fault, but I feel bad about your loss, anyway."

"Thanks be to El Señor Dios that the horses did not perish. At least there is that much to be grateful for." The hostler shook his head. "But your saddle, she is gone. All burned up."

"Is there a place in Los Pinos where I can buy another one?"

"Sí. The shop of Julio Montez. He makes fine saddles and will have some plain ones for sale, as well. But he can make one as fancy as you like, señor."

"I don't need fancy," Braddock said. "Just something I can ride."

A thought stirred in his head and made him narrow his eyes as he pondered again what John Edward Slattery had said. Maybe there was another way of looking at

Slattery's words. If Braddock was going to find out, he wouldn't be staying in Los Pinos for long.

Like it or not, as soon as he could manage it, he was headed back to Texas.

———

HE FORDED the Rio Grande about an hour after sunrise the next morning. He had been up early, before dawn, eating breakfast at the café where he'd had supper the previous night, before all the violence erupted. Then he had rousted Julio Montez from sleep and convinced the man to open his shop and sell Braddock a saddle and all the other tack he'd need. At least his saddlebags and Winchester had been safe in his hotel room, so he hadn't lost them in the blaze. The unexpected expenses had Braddock starting to run low on funds, though.

The dun had spent the night tied up in a small yard behind the hotel. The horse had come when Braddock whistled for him, after the fire. The two of them had been trail partners for a long time, so Braddock had been confident that the dun probably hadn't wandered far after stampeding out of the livery stable with the other mounts.

The local constable had proven to be as unambitious as Chuco had said. The man showed up to question Braddock about the fire and the dead man, but he had accepted without reservation Braddock's story that he had no idea who Slattery was or why he'd been shot. Braddock told the lawman that he had run into the stable when he saw the fire, found Slattery's body, and dragged it clear after freeing the horses so they wouldn't burn to death. Like the best lies, the story had a semblance of truth.

The townspeople with the fire wagon had saved most of the building. The roof would have to be repaired, but it hadn't collapsed. The walls were smoke-blackened but intact. The hayloft was gone, completely burned, as were some of the stalls. The smell of smoke would linger for quite a while. But the place could be put right again with time, effort, and money.

It was too bad the same couldn't be said of the past, mused Braddock as he rode out of the border river onto the soil of Texas once again.

He had been back in Texas numerous times since the legislature, in a fit of political posturing, had decided to strip the Rangers down to a bare minimum of men. Budget cutting, they called it, but like everything politicians did, in reality it was all about who had the power to impose their will and who didn't. The end result was that Braddock and lot of other good officers had lost their badges.

Braddock hadn't let that stop him from pursuing justice. More than once, he had ridden into some town where trouble was brewing and allowed the local authorities to believe that he was still a Ranger so they would cooperate with him. Such deception was against the law, of course, and had caused some hard feelings in Austin. But as Slattery had said, the Rangers who actually worked out in the field knew Braddock, knew what he was able to accomplish, and weren't going to get in a big hurry about tracking him down and arresting him.

Slattery had been on Braddock's mind a lot during the night, while he was trying to sleep. On the face of it, Slattery meeting with Montayne and the outlaw's comment about letting Slattery in on the plan made for an obvious conclusion: Slattery had gone bad and was joining the gang raising hell along the border.

Braddock didn't believe that for one damned second.

He was convinced that somehow, while investigating the case north of the border, Slattery had discovered that Montayne was connected to the gang. He had gotten on Montayne's trail and followed him to Los Pinos. He could have pretended to be an outlaw himself and worked his way into Montayne's confidence in an attempt to infiltrate the gang. Once Braddock put that theory together in his head, it made perfect sense and explained the rendezvous in the livery stable. Slattery, more than likely, wouldn't have been aware that Braddock was in the same town until that moment while the Ranger was dying, outside the burning stable.

And at that moment, Slattery had tried to tell Braddock something. Something important. But all he'd managed to do was tell him to go to the Devil and mentioned something about a hole. Or something holy. Or the whole of something equally mysterious. It had been a maddening dead end for Braddock at first.

Until he'd remembered hearing about a place called Devil's Hole. Slattery hadn't been telling him to go to the Devil. He'd been telling Braddock to go to Devil's Hole.

At least, that was what Braddock *hoped* Slattery had tried to tell him.

He had never been there, knew only vaguely where it was. Braddock had no idea what he'd find there, either, but it had to be something important enough for John Edward Slattery to cling to life as he tried to pass along the message.

Once Braddock had thought of Devil's Hole, a story had come back to him, one that he had heard his father tell when he was a boy. It involved John Coffee Hays, one of the first of the famous Texas Rangers back in the days when the Republic of Texas was its own country. Cap'n

Jack, as the men under his command called him, had been riding one day across an arid, inhospitable stretch of country. Finally, he had come to a deep hole with a ragged edge of rocks around it, and looking down into it, he had seen water at the bottom. It just so happened that a Mexican peasant had come along right then, and Cap'n Jack asked him what this place was called.

"San Pablo's Well, señor," the Mexican had told him.

"Saint Paul's, hell," Cap'n Jack had responded as he sniffed the air and caught a hint of sulphur rising from the opening. "It smells more like the Devil's Hole to me."

And so it had been called, ever since.

Braddock's lips curved in a faint smile as that memory played in his head. Like a lot of stories told in Texas, about Texas, by Texans, there might not be a lick of truth in it. But that didn't really matter, because there was truth in the real world and truth in an hombre's heart, and they didn't always match up perfect-like. But truth in the heart was more important.

He rode a little west of due north. South Texas might be a small area in proportion to the rest of the state, but it was mighty big compared to just about anywhere else. If his memory of the times he had seen it on a map wasn't playing tricks on him, Devil's Hole was a couple days' ride north of the border, somewhere in the vicinity of the settlement of Chapparal City, so called because of the low, thick brush that grew all over the area. Braddock had never been there, either, just heard stories about the place. Ranger lore said that twenty years earlier, rustlers had used the settlement as their base between raids on the vast cattle ranches along the Gulf Coast to the east.

Given its location, Chapparal City could serve just as well as the headquarters of the gang raiding to the south, along the border, even though in these early days of the new century, it was supposed to be a civilized, respectable place now.

All sorts of evil could hide in seemingly respectable places, thought Braddock as he rode northwest.

His years of trailing men on the dodge had taught him how to travel across the range without drawing attention to himself. He was on the other side of the situation now, so he took advantage of all the tricks he had learned from manhunting. He avoided the small settlements and the busy roads, instead following smaller trails and animal tracks through the chaparral as long as they went in the general direction he wanted to go.

The tough, rangy longhorns of this brush country had rebuilt Texas's shattered economy after the Civil War. Men who were equally tough and rangy— "brush poppers", some called them—had gathered the longhorns into herds and pointed them north, toward the markets in Kansas that were opening up with the arrival of the railroad. Those early cattle drives had given Texans a foothold on reclaiming their own destinies and pushing out the greedy northerners who had come down here to ravage what was left after the war.

Of course, those carpetbaggers and reconstructionists were just the latest in a long line of ravagers, going back to the Comanches and the Spanish *conquistadores* and extending in the other direction to the wave of rustlers, bank robbers, and other outlaws that had washed over the state, a blood-red tide that had been stemmed only partially by the Rangers. That fight continued today, with Braddock being part of it whether his status was official or not. As long as lawbreakers were plaguing Texas, Braddock would go after them.

He managed to avoid trouble during the day and

camped that night in a small clearing deep in the chapparal where his fire wouldn't be seen. He slept well,
knowing that the dun would alert him if anybody came
skulking around. Out here in the brush, he was probably
in more danger from javelinas, the savage, feral, razor-
tusked pigs that roamed this area, than he was from
anything else.

None of the beasts came around that night, however,
and the next morning Braddock was in the saddle and
moving again as soon as the eastern sky was gray enough
for him to see where he was going.

He rode into mid-afternoon, pausing now and then
to rest the dun, gnaw on some jerky from his saddlebags,
and wash it down with a few swallows of tepid water
from his canteen. At one point he had to rein in sharply
when an angry buzzing sound came from the brush up
ahead at the side of the trail. Braddock didn't want to
fire a shot and draw attention to himself unless he abso-
lutely had to, so he dismounted and threw dirt clods into
the brush until the snake got annoyed enough to stop
rattling and slither off, away from the trail.

"I don't like those varmints," he said aloud to the dun,
who tossed his head in apparent agreement.

Braddock rode on.

A while later, he spotted a few columns of smoke to
the east, a mile or more away. Most men wouldn't have
been keen-eyed enough to notice them. The smoke probably came from chimneys in Chaparral City, he thought.
He knew he had come far enough from the border to be
in the settlement's vicinity. Of course, he was steering by
instinct . . . but Braddock trusted his instincts.

That also meant he probably wasn't too far from
Devil's Hole. Braddock didn't know what he was looking

for, but John Edward Slattery had told him to go there. With any luck he would figure it out when he reached his destination.

He was thinking that he might be forced to stop avoiding people and find an isolated ranch or a trail with somebody traveling on it so he could ask where to find Devil's Hole. But before he got around to doing that, he heard something not far off that made him rein in and frown as he listened.

The first noise was the swift rataplan of hoofbeats from galloping horses, followed by raucous, excited whoops. A gunshot popped, then another. Somebody was being chased, Braddock decided, and he couldn't help but be curious about what was going on. He nudged the dun into motion again on the faint, narrow trail they had been following.

Within moments, they came out onto a larger trail, one almost wide enough to be called a road. Braddock spotted a cloud of dust where the trail curved out of sight to his left. That was the tail-end of the pursuit, he decided. He didn't hesitate to turn the dun and follow.

The pounding hoofbeats ahead of him soon stopped. He heard more yelling but no more shots. He slowed the dun from a lope to a walk, not wanting to barge right into something without knowing what he was coming up on.

The chapparal suddenly peeled back to form a roughly circular, open expanse maybe a quarter of a mile across. The ground, which was mostly flat as a table in these parts, actually sloped up a little to a raised area in the center of the big clearing. A number of irregularly spaced boulders formed a crude ring on top of the raised area.

From the descriptions he had heard, he was looking at the Devil's Hole, Braddock realized.

He wasn't the only one here. Five horses stood riderless not far from the rocks, one apart and four together. Four men had been chasing one, and they had caught him here. Two of the pursuers stood to the side with drawn guns, while the other two gripped the arms of their quarry, a short, stocky man dressed in rough clothing.

"You know what to do, boys," one of the gunmen drawled.

The two captors dragged their prisoner forward, through a gap in the boulders. The man cried out and struggled frantically, but he couldn't break free. Braddock stiffened as he realized what they were about to do.

He drew his gun, but he was too late. He watched in horror as the two men threw their screaming captive into the Devil's Hole.

13

BRADDOCK'S FIRST IMPULSE WAS TO DRAW HIS GUN AND start shooting at the men. He held off, not because he was outnumbered four to one, but because he noticed something else.

A rope that had been tossed on the ground was looped around a rock slab and appeared to be tied securely. In his shock, Braddock hadn't noticed the captive being tied to a rope, but it seemed that might be the case.

The rope snapped taut after only a second. The screaming continued inside the Devil's Hole, echoing now. The man who'd been tossed in there was fortunate. The rope hadn't broken. He was dangling by it, down there in that hole.

Braddock was out in the open, and, not surprisingly, one of the gunmen noticed him. The man turned quickly toward Braddock and swung his gun around.

Braddock's Colt whispered out of its holster and rose, too. He wasn't going to let anybody shoot him out of the saddle without fighting back. And anybody cruel enough to order a man thrown into such a hole in the earth might try to kill a stranger for no good reason.

The other three men followed the first one's lead. They drew their guns, as well, but nobody fired. Braddock's sights were lined on the first man, and it was pretty obvious that even if they blew holes in him, he would kill at least one of them.

"Who the hell are you, mister?" the gunman demanded.

"I could ask the same," said Braddock, his voice a cool drawl that testified he wasn't afraid of them. "I'm also curious why you tossed that poor hombre into the hole."

"That's our business, not yours. In these parts, a man's wise to mind his own. Business, that is."

"I've found that to be true just about everywhere," Braddock said. "Still, this isn't something you see every day."

The man in the hole had fallen silent except for an occasional terrified whimper.

The spokesman inclined his head toward the Devil's Hole and asked, "Is that greaser a friend of yours, mister?"

"I don't even know who he is," Braddock answered honestly. "I didn't get a very good look at him before your friends pitched him in. Anyway, I don't know anybody in this part of the country."

"So you see, that's all the more reason for you to holster that gun, turn around, and ride away from here. Otherwise . . . well, Pancho there might have some company."

Braddock shook his head slowly. "Not likely."

"I didn't say you'd be *alive* when we toss you in there—"

Some racket in the brush on the other side of the

clearing interrupted the gunman's threat. The tension between Braddock and the four men was so thick, however, that none of them turned to look. Braddock, from his angle, was the only one who could see another rider push out of the brush. The newcomer wore tight black trousers and a bright blue shirt with a short charro jacket over it. A red sash was tied around his waist. A pearl gray sombrero was on his head, secured by a tight chin strap. As his horse took a couple of steps into the open, the man worked the lever of the Winchester in his hands. The sound it made was unmistakable.

"You're kind of stuck between a rock and a hard place, gents," the newcomer said in unaccented English. "You still have the numbers on your side, but I reckon being caught in a crossfire kind of balances that out."

The spokesman for the gunmen didn't turn around, but his jaw clenched so tightly that Braddock saw a little muscle in it jump.

"Somebody else who doesn't know how to keep his nose out of other people's business."

"I've been accused of it in the past," the newcomer said with a trace of mockery in his voice. "Now, since you boys seem to be fond of throwing things, why don't you throw your guns off into the brush? Nice and hard now, so they'll carry a ways."

One of the other men said, "Why don't you just go to hell, you—"

The Winchester blasted. The hat flew off the head of the man who'd been blustering. Before an echo of the gunshot could even begin to form, the man in the pearl gray sombrero had worked the rifle's lever and had another cartridge in the chamber.

"I can aim a little lower next time."

The leader of the gunmen cursed and told the others,

"Do what he says, damn it." He drew back his arm and sailed the gun he was holding into a spinning flight that carried it well into the chaparral. One by one, the others followed suit.

"Now pull that man out of there before his heart gives out on him," the rifleman ordered. "And be mighty careful about it. If he was to fall, I wouldn't take it kindly."

The four men bent to the rope and started hauling the man out of the Devil's Hole. Braddock drifted closer on the dun, until he was able to see that the hole was about forty feet in diameter. He had no idea how deep it was, but judging by how the man's screams had echoed, it went down a good distance into the earth. A couple of hundred feet, maybe.

It didn't take long for the men to pull the prisoner back to the surface. The rope had only allowed him to fall ten or twelve feet. Even so, they were red-faced and grunting from the effort by the time they were done. Lifting a grown man's dead weight could be a chore, and the man they had thrown in the hole was stocky enough that he wasn't light.

The leader said, "Crawford, get his feet. Be careful you don't fall in."

The gunman called Crawford looked plenty worried as he got down on his knees at the edge of the hole and leaned forward to grasp the prisoner's ankle that had the rope tied around it. As the other three men lifted the captive a little higher, Crawford got hold of the other ankle and hauled up and back as hard as he could. He fell backwards as the captive came out of the hole. As soon as the man could get his hands on the ground, he scrambled to get clear. When Crawford let go of him, he crawled frantically for several yards. Then he lay face down, spread eagled, digging his fingers and toes into the ground as if he would never let go.

The captive's feet were bare, Braddock noted. He wore the pajama-like garb of a Mexican farmer. He was still whimpering, even though he was out of the Devil's Hole.

The rifleman called across the clearing to Braddock, "You need these boys for anything else?"

"Not that I can think of."

The rifleman nodded and motioned with the Winchester's barrel to the four men. "Get on your horses and get out of here, while you've got the chance."

"Our guns—" one of them began.

"You can come back and look for them later, if you're of a mind to." The rifleman lifted the Winchester. "Don't go making me regret that I'm feeling generous."

The leader of the bunch glared and said, "There'll be another day."

"I expect you're right about that. The sun seems to be in the habit of coming up in the morning."

The four gunmen climbed into their saddles. Braddock moved the dun around the edge of the chaparral so he wouldn't be blocking the trail. They cast dark, murderous glances at him, too, as they rode out. They disappeared around a bend in the trail where it curved through the chaparral.

"We'd better stay alert," Braddock said. "I didn't see rifles on any of their saddles, but some of them could have spare Colts in their saddlebags."

"You keep an eye out for them," the man said as he slid his Winchester back in its sheath. "I want to check on that poor hombre who got tossed in the hole."

Braddock dismounted and pulled his rifle from its scabbard. He walked toward the hole in the ground and stepped up onto the rock slab to which the rope was tied. In country like this, even a slight elevation was enough to allow a fella to see a long way. He looked in the direction the four men had ridden off. He spotted them in the distance, heading east now.

Meanwhile, the man in the gray sombrero knelt beside the man who had been thrown in the hole and spoke to him in a low voice. Braddock couldn't make out the words, but he could tell the man was speaking Spanish. Fluently, from the sound of it.

The victim of the cruel act sat up, slowly, shakily, urged on by the man kneeling beside him. The man in the sombrero put a hand on his shoulder to steady him. They spoke together, quietly. Braddock heard the murmurs while he watched the dust haze left by the departing riders. It dwindled as they got farther away, until he couldn't see it anymore.

He turned and said, "They're gone."

"You're sure of that, friend?" asked the man in the gray sombrero as he looked up at Braddock.

"Well, I suppose they could be playing a trick of some sort and intend to double back, but they didn't show any signs of it."

"Sidewinders like that, it's hard to tell what they might do."

Braddock stepped down from the rock and tucked his Winchester under his left arm. "That's true," he admitted.

"They . . . they will be back," said the man dressed like a farmer. "They do not have what they want yet. They will return until they do."

The man in the gray sombrero straightened to his feet and extended a hand to the other. "Let's get you up, amigo," he said. "A man standing can get his nerve back easier than one sitting down."

The farmer hesitated, then clasped the man's hand and allowed himself to be helped to his feet. Looking a little ashamed, he brushed off his simple clothing.

"I should not have run," he muttered. "I should have told them to get off my land. But they took me by surprise, and I was frightened." He shrugged. "Besides, I have no gun."

"It's the Twentieth Century," Braddock said. "Modern times. A law-abiding man shouldn't have to pack a gun to protect himself."

The man in the sombrero laughed. "That's a pretty thought, isn't it, my friend? But when the century changed, it didn't work any magic. People are still people. And that means most of them are out for what they can get, no matter what it takes to get it."

"That's kind of a bleak outlook on life, isn't it?" asked Braddock, while not actually disagreeing with what the stranger had said.

"I prefer to think of it as a practical outlook." The man held out his hand and introduced himself. "I'm Francisco Rojas."

Now that he'd gotten a better look at the man, Braddock had noted already that he was Mexican, young and dark-haired with dashing good looks. That went with the outfit he wore, but Braddock was a little surprised, anyway, because Rojas spoke English with no trace of an accent.

That might have been a giveaway in itself, Braddock realized as he shook hands with Rojas and felt the iron strength in the long, slender fingers. Rojas didn't have a Mexican accent, but he didn't sound at all like a Texan, either.

Braddock supplied his name and added, "I'm guessing you learned to speak English at school."

A grin flashed across Rojas's face. "Not really, but I spent a few years at Washington University in St. Louis and sort of lost my accent. My father thought some higher education would do me good. The jury's still out on whether he was right or not." Rojas nodded toward the other man. "This is Juan Belmosa."

"The two of you are acquainted?"

"Not at all. Juan just introduced himself to me. I never laid eyes on him until those sons of bitches pulled him out of that hole. Well, that's not strictly true. I caught a glimpse of him just as they pitched him in, as I'm guessing you did."

"*El agujero del Diablo*," Juan Belmosa said with a look of fear in his eyes again.

"The Devil's Hole. A fitting name." Rojas turned to study the opening in the earth. Braddock did likewise. Juan just edged a little farther away from it.

Rojas moved closer. So did Braddock. He said, "How deep is it, do you reckon?"

"A hundred and fifty feet? Two hundred?" Rojas shook his head. "Plenty deep enough that a man could never climb out of it, even if the fall didn't kill him, which it would. And there's usually water standing in the bottom of it, according to Juan, so if by some miracle a fella survived the fall, chances are he'd drown."

"So it's deadly in more ways than one."

"Like a lot of other things in life," Rojas said with a sardonic smile.

"What do you think causes a thing like this?"

"I studied geology and natural science at the university. It has to do with subterranean water supplies and the different strata of the earth. Or, you could just say that God reached down and poked a hole in the ground with His finger. Either explanation will do for practical purposes. What matters is that, according to Juan, some fellas around here have been putting it to pretty grim use."

Braddock frowned and asked, "Meaning?"

"Juan's not the first one who got thrown into the Devil's Hole. But in all likelihood, he's the first one who's survived that fate."

Braddock turned and looked at Juan Belmosa, who shrugged and nodded.

"*Es verdad, señor,*" he said. "The bones of several of my amigos rest at the bottom. If you come with me to my home, I will be happy to tell you all about it."

"I reckon I'll take you up on that," Braddock said. "That sounds like a story I want to hear."

"As do I," Francisco Rojas added.

JUAN BELMOSA'S HOUSE, which was not a *jacal* but rather a decent-sized adobe dwelling, was about three-quarters of a mile away from the Devil's Hole.

"I do not like living so close to such an evil place," he said to Braddock and Rojas as they rode toward the farm, "and I especially do not like my family living there, but it was the land I could get, and a man must have land if he is to till the soil." The farmer shrugged. "And it is not *bad* land, you understand. If there was better water, I know I could grow a great many crops, instead of the few I struggle to produce."

Belmosa had limped heavily as he walked to his horse, so much so that Rojas had to help him. The rope had wrenched heavily on his ankle when his plummeting weight reached the end of it. But considering the alternative, it was an injury that the middle-aged man would gladly suffer.

When they rode up to the farm, which had a shed for a pair of mules, an attached corral, a vegetable garden, and a small chicken pen, several children ran out to greet them and swarmed around Belmosa, accompanied by a pair of yapping dogs. A sternly attractive woman about Belmosa's age emerged from the house and met them, as well.

"Did something happen?" she asked Belmosa bluntly. "I thought I heard men shouting and shots in the distance."

"Four men surprised me in the fields," he told her. He dismounted and gave her a hug as if he'd thought that he would never see her again. For a few seconds there, that had come all too close to being true. "They chased me, frightened me. But these men came and helped me."

He turned and nodded toward Braddock and Rojas. He didn't say anything about being thrown in the Devil's Hole. On the way here, he had told his two new friends that he didn't want to mention it in front of the children, because it might scare them too much to know how close he had come to dying.

"Señores," the woman said with a grave nod. "*Muchas gracias* for helping my Juan." She held out a hand toward the house. "Please, enjoy the hospitality of my home."

"We are obliged to you, señora," Rojas said as he swept off his hat and bowed low to her.

"Ma'am," Braddock said. He nodded and pinched the brim of his hat.

They followed Belmosa, his wife, and the swarm of children and dogs inside.

Over a simple but appetizing supper of beans,

tortillas, and stew, Belmosa explained, "This was a good place to live until a few months ago. A challenging place, but good. A man could make a decent living for his family if he was willing to work. The ranches, they flourished, too. Then the bandits came, raiding the towns, stealing cattle, burning barns, killing anyone who tried to stop them."

"Raiders from the other side of the border?" asked Rojas.

Belmosa made a face and waved his hands. "Did those men today look like *Mejicanos?*"

"As a matter of fact," said Braddock, "they were all gringos, as far as I could tell."

"And that is the truth," Belmosa responded vehemently. "At first, they pretended to be those of my race. In fact, some of them actually may have been Mexican. But not all."

Rojas leaned back in his chair and sipped from the cup of coffee señora Belmosa had poured for him. "Greed knows no skin color or race," he said. "Men filled with avarice will work with whoever can help them get what they want."

Braddock nodded and said, "I reckon that's true most of the time."

What Belmosa was telling them fit right in with the idea that had been stirring around in Braddock's mind ever since John Edward Slattery had told him about the outbreak of lawlessness along the Rio Grande. Get the Texans to blame the Mexicans and the Mexicans to blame the Texans, and that would muddy the waters and make it more difficult to run the outlaws to ground on either side of the border. One gang, switching hats and outer clothes and riding back and forth across the river . . .

"But in recent weeks things have become worse," Belmosa continued. "The attacks are more frequent, more out in the open. Those men today, they did not even bother pretending to be anything other than what they were: gringo outlaws."

"But what are they after, other than loot?" asked Braddock. "Is there some other goal?"

Belmosa shrugged. "Some people have received warnings that if they do not leave, they and their families will be killed. The men today said they would teach me a lesson, so my family would know they can no longer stay here."

"That's why you said they would be back," Rojas said.

"They will not leave until they have what they want," Belmosa said solemnly. "And as far as I can tell from the terror they have inflicted, that is the entire valley of the Rio Grande."

14

Belmosa offered Braddock and Rojas the room he and his wife shared, but Braddock insisted that the shed would do fine. The weather was pleasant, with no sign of rain.

"I've spent a lot of nights out on the trail," Braddock said. "So this won't bother me at all."

Rojas laughed. "You shame me into the same response, my friend. How can I put our kind hosts out of their own bed when you refuse to do so?"

"Don't let me make up your mind for you," Braddock told him.

Rojas waved a hand and said, "No, no, it's fine." He gave a half-bow to señora Belmosa. "My thanks to you for such a fine meal and for being so gracious to us, señora."

"De nada, señor," the woman murmured.

The horses and mules were turned out into the corral for the night. Braddock and Rojas spread their bedrolls on a pile of clean straw and stretched out. Rojas took a slender black cigarillo from his pocket and flicked a match to life to light it.

"You'd best not go to sleep with that thing burning," Braddock said. "We're liable to have a blaze in here if you do."

"Don't worry, G.W.," Rojas replied familiarly. "I'm pretty wide awake. I don't expect to doze off any time soon."

"Thinking about what's been happening around here?"

"It's hard not to, after seeing what those fellows did to poor Juan, and now, after meeting his family, I'm angrier than ever. These people don't have much. No one has the right to come along and try to take it away from them."

"No, I reckon not," Braddock agreed. "I'm guessing you come from a pretty well-to-do family, yourself."

"What makes you think that?" asked Rojas as he puffed a cloud of gray smoke toward the shed roof.

"Well, you said your father sent you to that university in St. Louis. I figure something like that costs plenty of money."

"He can afford it," Rojas responded casually. "He has a large ranch south of here, down on the border."

"In Mexico?"

"No. My family are *Tejanos*, G.W. We were ranching down there on the Rio Grande before Moses Austin ever even heard of Texas. The spread is twenty miles or so up the river from Brownsville. That's where I was headed when I ran into you and Juan at the Devil's Hole." Rojas puffed on the cigarillo for a moment, then added, "Now I'm thinking I may stay around these parts for a while."

"That could be dangerous," Braddock pointed out.

"Those fellas warned us that they'd see us again and that we shouldn't poke around in other folks' business."

"And I'm sure you always do everything you're told," said Rojas.

"Well . . . not always. Not often, if we're being honest. I thought I might ride over to Chapparal City in the morning and take a look around."

"You think you might find something interesting?"

"A fella never knows until he tries."

Rojas chuckled. "That's true. Feel like having some company on the ride?"

"Sure, I'd be glad to have you come along . . . provided you don't set the place on fire between now and then."

Rojas laughed again, snuffed out the cigarillo's glowing end between middle finger and thumb, and tossed the butt well out of the shed onto bare dirt.

"Will you sleep better now, G.W.?"

"I expect that depends on whether or not you snore," Braddock said.

BRADDOCK SLEPT ALL RIGHT, so he supposed Francisco Rojas didn't snore, or not enough to bother him, anyway. In the morning, they had breakfast with the Belmosa family and then bid them farewell, saddling up and riding southeast toward Chapparal City.

"Part of me feels like we should have stayed around for a while, in case those hombres come back and try to cause more trouble," Braddock commented as the two riders moved along easily.

"The same thought occurred to me," Rojas said, "but we can't just stay there from now on. Anyway, if they're keeping an eye on the place, maybe we'll draw them off by leaving." He grinned. "They have a grudge against the two of us, G.W. I'm betting they'll want to settle it."

"Wouldn't be surprised."

Braddock kept his eyes open as he rode, scanning the surrounding countryside for any signs of potential trouble. Of course, in this flat, brushy country, there was a limit to how much a man could see. Enemies could be lurking almost anywhere in the chapparal.

"What did you study at that university?" Braddock asked to pass the time as they rode.

"Besides women and race horses and poker hands, you mean?" Rojas laughed. "A little of this and a little of that. I never could seem to settle on any one thing. Once I learned a little about a subject, I got interested in something else. How about you, G.W.?"

"You mean, did I go to college?" Braddock shook his head. "No, I never got around to it. I did all right in school as a youngster, I suppose, but, like you, I was more interested in other things."

Like hunting down outlaws, he thought. Growing up as the son of a Texas Ranger, that was all he'd ever wanted to do.

And the state had tried to take that away from him. Not much chance of that!

At mid-morning, they stopped to rest the horses and let them drink from a small creek that twisted through the chapparal close to the trail. Rojas hunkered on his heels next to the stream and reached down to scoop up a handful of water.

As he did, a sudden crashing in the brush heralded the arrival of trouble. Rojas twisted around as a large javelina erupted from the thick growth only a few yards away from him. When he turned, one foot slipped out from under him in the mud at the edge of the creek, and he sat down awkwardly, half in and half out of the water, as the tusker charged him.

Braddock was standing beside the dun while the horses drank. He whirled to face the threat, too. The javelina was a big one, a couple of feet tall, probably four feet from tail to snout, and weighing around eighty pounds, Braddock guessed. Certainly big enough to inflict some real damage on Rojas—unless Braddock could stop it.

His Colt seemed to leap out of its holster into his hand. The big revolver boomed four times. Braddock aimed all four shots at the javelina's head. He knew the slugs would most likely bounce off the brute's thick skull, but one of them might penetrate the beady eye and bore all the way into the javelina's brain. That was the fastest way to bring it down. Shots to the body would kill the creature eventually, but it would have time to savage Rojas before it died.

Luck and skill combined to guide Braddock's bullets. One of them found the javelina's right eye. The animal's momentum carried it forward, but now its head drooped and there was no living brain controlling its muscles. Its front legs folded under it, and the javelina's snout plowed into the dirt as it came to a shuddering stop less than a yard from Rojas, who stared wide-eyed at the beast.

"What . . . what a monster!" Rojas exclaimed when he found his voice after a moment. "He would have killed me." He looked at Braddock. "We are even now, my friend—"

More crashing nearby in the brush interrupted him. Braddock holstered his gun and said, "Come on! We need to get out of here."

Rojas scrambled to his feet and lunged toward his

horse. Braddock was already swinging up into the saddle on the dun. In addition to the sound of bodies breaking through the chapparal, both men heard loud, guttural grunting and knew it came from more of the javelinas.

As soon as Braddock pulled the dun around, he understood why a large group of the tuskers were stampeding toward them. A wind from the west blew the smell of smoke into his face. He saw the smoke itself, thick white clouds of the stuff, rising from the landscape several hundred yards away. At the base of the smoke wall, flames jumped up and down wildly.

"They've set the chapparal on fire!" Braddock called to Rojas. The blaze spread as far as he could see in both directions. It roared toward them like a freight train.

"We need to get out of here!" Rojas said.

They turned their horses just as a dozen or more javelinas seemed to explode out of the brush. The beasts were terrified of the onrushing fire, but their instincts also made them want to attack the horses. Braddock knew those sharp tusks could sever tendons and cripple horses. He jammed his boot heels into the dun's flanks and sent the horse leaping ahead into a gallop. Rojas was right beside him.

Since the javelinas were much lower to the ground, they could move faster in the brush, but on the open trail the horses were able to outrun them. Rojas looked back over his shoulder as they left the creatures behind and said with a grin, "There's going to be some fried pig in these parts today!"

"Yeah, but it's not their fault," replied Braddock. "I reckon the varmints who set that fire are after us!"

And with all those flames behind them, there was only one way to go: straight ahead. Which meant it was likely somebody would be waiting for them up there . . .

That thought had just crossed Braddock's mind when gunfire crashed from the chaparral. Rojas cried out as his horse stumbled and collapsed in a violent, rolling fall. He would have been crushed, more than likely, if he hadn't kicked his feet free in time. He sailed over the horse's head, instead, and came down hard in the middle of the trail.

Braddock had reined in by the time Rojas landed. He whipped his Winchester out and returned the fire, swinging the rifle from left to right as he cranked off five rounds as swiftly as he could work the lever. He had seen the muzzle flashes in the growth where the bush-whackers lurked, so he sprayed lead in that area. If nothing else, he might distract them for a moment.

He brought the dun alongside the stunned Rojas and held the Winchester in his left hand as he extended the right to the young *Tejano*. "Francisco!" he said urgently, trying to penetrate the fog in Rojas's brain.

Rojas shook his head, looked up, and saw Braddock's hand. His expression cleared as he reached up and clasped Braddock's wrist.

"My horse?" he asked.

"Done for," Braddock said as he hauled Rojas up behind him.

Braddock's accurate rifle fire must have forced the bushwhackers to dive to the ground, because their guns had fallen silent. But that respite ended quickly, as more shots lanced out from the chaparral. Braddock heard the slugs whipping past him as he drove the dun forward. Guiding the horse with his knees, he brought the Winchester to his shoulder and opened fire again.

Rojas joined in the fight with his revolver. The gun boomed behind Braddock, the reports slamming painfully into his ears. He wasn't worried as much about that, however, as he was about escaping from this trap of flame and lead.

Braddock bent low in the saddle to make himself a smaller target. Rojas did likewise behind him. For a second, Braddock considered veering off the trail into the chapparal. That wouldn't work, he decided. The clinging growth would slow them down, and neither he nor Rojas wore the leather chaps and jackets of the brush poppers. The thorny branches would claw them to ribbons if they went very far, to say nothing of doing the same to Braddock's horse.

The bushwhack lead had been coming from the left side of the trail. Now more shots roared from the right. Braddock bit back a curse and hauled on the reins. With gunmen lurking on both sides of the trail, there was no way he and Rojas would survive trying to run that gauntlet.

Grimacing, Braddock wheeled the dun around and started back the way they had come from. More bullets whined around them. Rojas yelled, "What are you doing? The whole world's on fire this way!"

"We didn't have a chance in that crossfire!" Braddock said over his shoulder. "We'll just have to find a way through the flames."

He heard Rojas mutter something about him being loco. Braddock couldn't argue with that assessment. But sometimes, if a man got in a bad enough fix, "loco" was the only way out.

He remembered the creek where they had encountered the first javelina a short time earlier. The stream wasn't very big, but it might be better than nothing.

To get there, they had to pass the horse that had been shot out from under Rojas. As they drew near it, the

Tejano pounded on Braddock's shoulder and shouted, "Stop! Let me get my saddlebags!"

Braddock started to refuse. Every moment might mean the difference between life and death for them. But he knew that if the tables were turned, he would want to salvage as much of his outfit as he could.

He drew back on the reins as they reached the fallen horse. "Hurry!" he called to Rojas, who slipped down from the dun's back before the mount had even stopped moving. He landed running and dashed to the other horse's side.

Fortunately, the saddlebags hadn't gotten pinned under the carcass. If they had, Rojas would have been forced to abandon them. As it was, he was able to get them loose in a matter of seconds.

Just as he straightened with the pair of connected saddlebags in his hand, more shots rang out. Braddock felt the wind-rip of a slug past his cheek. He looked around and saw that several mounted men had just rounded a bend in the trail and were charging toward them. Smoke and flame jetted from the guns the men held.

"Come on!" he yelled to Rojas, who vaulted onto the dun's back behind him, landing with a pained grunt. Braddock kicked the horse into a run again.

He mentally cursed himself for stopping. Not only had the bushwhackers nearly caught up with them, but there was also a chance that the raging flames had blocked their access to the creek by now.

"Those sons of bitches chasing us are wearing masks!" Rojas said. "It's the same bunch that's been raising hell around here!"

Braddock didn't doubt that for a second. The men must have been watching Juan Belmosa's farm and had seen him and Rojas leave, then moved quickly to set up this trap in the chaparral. Braddock had wanted to draw the ravagers away from the Belmosa family. It appeared he had succeeded in that, anyway.

The wind was still blowing, but its speed had died down a little. That was the only shred of hope left for Braddock to cling to. Between the way the dun was galloping, and the flames that were advancing, the gap closed quickly. Smoke thickened in the air, choking Braddock and Rojas and making both men cough. The dun kept running, but it slowed as the smoke began to affect it, too.

"We have to get out of this!" Rojas shouted.

"Hang on!" Braddock told him as the dun rounded a bend in the twisting trail. There weren't many landmarks in this flat, brushy country, but he saw how the chaparral thinned out, up ahead on the right, and thought that might be where the creek was.

Unfortunately, the brush was burning on both side of the trail just beyond that.

The dun skidded and shied as every instinct in its body screamed for it to turn and flee. Braddock tightened his grip on the reins and fought to bring the horse under control. They were wasting valuable seconds.

At least the men chasing them had fallen back, so nobody was shooting at them anymore. Those hombres must have figured the flames would get them, thought Braddock. And they might be right, yet . . .

He jabbed his heels into the dun's flanks and forced the horse into the chaparral on the right. The prickly stuff clawed at them, but the growth was thin enough that the dun was able to batter down a path. The fire was so close that the flames weren't really crackling anymore. It was more of a roaring sound, almost like a

136

train or a tornado bearing down on them. The smoke wrapped around them so thoroughly that Braddock couldn't see ten feet in front of him, couldn't seem to get any breath into his lungs.

Then, with no warning, water splashed up around the dun's hooves. Braddock reined in. Between wracking coughs, he said to Rojas, "Get . . . down! Get . . . in the creek!"

Rojas practically fell off the horse. He landed face down in the stream and was soaked instantly. The creek was about ten feet wide, maybe a foot and a half deep.

Braddock threw himself out of the saddle. He dragged hard at the reins, trying to get the dun to lie down. The horse was panic-stricken and didn't want to cooperate. Braddock was afraid he might have to let go and allow the dun to fend for itself in order to save his own life, but just as he was about to reach that terrible decision, the horse went along with him and lay down in the creek. Braddock stretched out in the water alongside his trail partner, still clinging to the reins.

He pulled his bandana from his pocket, made sure it was good and soaked, and clumsily tied it around his head so the wet cloth covered his mouth and nose. That helped a little with the smoke, which still stung his eyes. When he looked around at Rojas, he saw that the man had a bright yellow scarf tied around his head.

"Keep your head under as much as you can!" he shouted over the roar of the fire. "Just come up and get a breath when you have to!"

Rojas nodded and plunged his head under the surface. Braddock did the same. He wished he could have fastened some sort of mask around the horse's nose, but there was no time for that. The fire was all around them, flames rising up on both sides of the creek and seeming to swallow the whole world.

The water ought to keep them from burning to death, Braddock knew, but that didn't mean they would survive. More than once, he had heard stories about men being trapped in prairie fires who had avoided the flames but died anyway because the blaze consumed all the air around them. That was a possibility here. Braddock hoped he and Rojas were low enough to the ground that they might be able to breathe enough to keep them alive.

One thing was for sure, he thought. He had a better idea now what hell would be like, if that was where he wound up.

15

ALTHOUGH THE NIGHTMARISH BLAZE SEEMED ENDLESS, IN reality the flames rolled on past Braddock and Rojas in a matter of minutes. The racket died down, the smoke began to thin, and Braddock knew he had made it through the ordeal. The dun tossed its head a little, letting Braddock know that his old friend was still alive, as well.

What about Rojas? Braddock's eyes were watering so much from the smoke that he couldn't see much of anything. He lifted his head and called softly through the soaked bandana, "Francisco!"

"Huh . . . Here," came the feeble reply. "G.W.?"

"I'm here," Braddock told him. Their voices were both so hoarse and raspy that it sounded painful just to hear them talk. At least it did to Braddock's ears.

He pushed himself to a sitting position. Rojas was a few feet away, struggling to sit up as well. Braddock scooped up water in his hand and used to wash his eyes. That relieved some of the discomfort. He took off the bandana, wrung it out, and wiped his face and eyes.

Then he drank some of the water to soothe his burning throat.

Splashing, the dun rose on all four legs. Braddock's sight was improving. He studied the horse and decided that the dun had made it through relatively unharmed. There were a few angry red spots on the sleek hide where embers had landed and caused small burns.

Rojas coughed and splashed water on his face, too. He managed to say, "We should go. Those men may still come looking for us."

"I was just thinking the same thing," Braddock agreed. "They're going to have a hard time sneaking up on us, though."

"What do you . . . Oh, I understand."

Both men got to their feet and looked around. Some of the brush had burned completely. In other places, the flames had consumed all the leaves but left blackened branches that twisted grotesquely and almost looked like they were writhing around. Those charred bushes didn't provide much cover. Braddock and Rojas could see pretty well for hundreds of yards around them, on both sides of the creek.

The stream ran roughly north and south. Braddock nodded to the north and said, "I reckon we ought to go that way. And we should walk in the creek because the ground out there's probably still pretty hot."

"I agree with that," said Rojas, "but if we head north, we may run into the men who set the fire."

"If we go south, those bushwhackers may be waiting for us."

Rojas shrugged. "The old damned if we do, damned if we don't conundrum, eh?"

"You're an odd bird for the son of a *Tejano* ranchero, you know that?"

"So I've been told. But after considering your suggestion, I agree that we should go north. There seems less chance of running into trouble that way. The men who set the fire probably circled around it to rejoin the rest of the gang."

"That's what I figure. What I'm hoping, anyway." Braddock caught hold of the dun's dangling reins, which he had dropped while he was tending to his eyes. "Let's go."

They waded along the creek with Braddock leading the dun. The smell of burned vegetation was still strong and unpleasant in the air, although the steady breeze from the west helped dispel it to a certain extent. Rojas coughed a couple of times and said, "Damn. I think I'm going to be coughing up ashes for a month. And that chapparal scratched the hell out of me before we found the creek."

"It was pretty bad," Braddock agreed, "but we're alive."

"That's more than I expected would be true," said Rojas. "I thought we were finished, G.W. We would have been, if not for your quick thinking."

Braddock chuckled. "Sometimes a man may seem pretty smart, but the truth of it is that he's been backed so far into a corner, there's nothing else left for him to do."

"You can look at it like that if you want to, but I believe in giving credit where credit is due."

"Don't worry about credit. Just keep your eyes peeled for more of that masked bunch."

After a while they reached the edge of the burned area, where the fire had been started. They were still about a mile southeast of Juan Belmosa's farm, Braddock realized to his relief. The worry that the outlaws might have gone after Belmosa again had been lurking in the back of his mind.

"Say, do you think Juan might be willing to loan me his horse?" asked Rojas as they walked out of the creek. "That way, we wouldn't have to ride double all the way to Chapparal City."

"The same thought occurred to me," Braddock said, nodding. He swung up onto the dun and held out his hand to Rojas. "Come on. I want to check on them, anyway."

"I agree," Rojas said. He climbed onto the dun's back behind Braddock. "Maybe we should have tried to convince them to come into town with us where they'd be safer."

Braddock shook his head. "I don't reckon Juan would have left his place like that. From what I could tell, he's got a pretty stubborn streak in him."

It didn't take them long to ride to the Belmosa farm. As they approached, the dogs came out to bark at them. Braddock didn't see anybody else moving around the place, though. A feeling of unease stirred inside him.

"I don't like this," Rojas said, revealing that he felt the same way.

Grim-faced, Braddock kept the dun moving until they were close enough to hear sounds coming through the open door from inside the adobe house. Somebody in there was sobbing.

Rojas cursed quietly. "The bastards came back here after all. We should have stayed—"

"We talked about that," Braddock said. "Stayed for how long? From now on?"

"Until somebody does something about those bandits and killers!"

Braddock turned his head to look over his shoulder.

"Who's going to do something about them?" he asked coolly.

"Well . . . I was starting to think that maybe you and I would."

"So was I. And to do that, we have to find them, and find out who's behind them. We couldn't do that here."

Rojas sighed. "I know. I suppose I just wish there was a way to be in two places at once." He drew in a deep breath. "We'd better go find out how bad it is."

"I'll do that. You check around the place, make sure none of the varmints are waiting to ambush us."

"Don't you think they would have done it by now if they were going to?"

"Maybe. Maybe they want us to get a little closer."

"They're probably convinced we burned up in that fire."

"More than likely," Braddock said. "But let's make sure."

"Sort of free in giving the orders, aren't you, amigo?"

"Then you can go and see why señora Belmosa is crying."

Rojas shook his head at that suggestion. He slipped down from the dun's back and drew his gun. "I'll have that look around."

"Yell if you run into any trouble."

"Oh, I will, you can count on that."

Braddock nudged the dun into motion again and rode slowly toward the house. Inside, the sobbing continued. He dismounted near the front door, rested his hand on the butt of his Colt, and stepped into the opening.

Instantly, he saw one of the Belmosa children, a boy about ten years old, struggling to lift a shotgun and point it at him. Braddock held out his left hand, palm toward the boy, and said, "Hold it, son. I mean you no harm. I was just here earlier this morning, remember?"

He took in the scene. Señora Belmosa sat at the table, slumping forward with her head resting on her arms as her back shook from the sobs that wracked her. The other children were gathered around her, except for the boy who appeared to have appointed himself their guardian. All the youngsters looked scared and sad. The girls were sniffling. So was one of the younger boys.

Señora Belmosa raised her head, saw Braddock, and said to the boy with the shotgun, "No, Paco. This man is a friend."

Braddock wasn't sure just how good of a friend he really was. He hadn't seen hide nor hair of Juan Belmosa and was afraid that something had happened to the farmer.

Since there was no getting around it, he asked, "Where's your husband, señora?"

"They . . . they took him. Men with masks on their faces."

"Gringos?"

Señora Belmosa shook her head helplessly, unable to answer the question.

Paco had lowered the shotgun so that the twin barrels pointed toward the floor, but he didn't let go of the weapon. He spoke up and said, "I can tell you, señor Braddock. Some of the men were gringos. But some were *Mejicanos*. I could tell when they spoke to each other. And all of them were evil."

"I can't argue with you there, son," Braddock said. "They took your father?"

"Sí. He . . . he tried to fight them, but they hit him with their guns and knocked him down. Then they picked him up and tied his hands together in front of him and tied him to a saddle. When they rode off, he had to run to keep up with them. They . . . they laughed at him."

The boy's voice shook a little with rage.

"Which way did they go?"

It was señora Belmosa who answered. "Toward *el agujero del Diablo*," she said and then, another wail came from her.

The outlaws had taken Juan Belmosa back to the Devil's Hole. Braddock wasn't surprised by that. He'd been expecting it, in fact, ever since he and Rojas had ridden up and realized that something was wrong here.

At that moment, Rojas stepped into the open doorway and reported, "The place is empty except for the livestock, G.W. Doesn't look the bas—the varmints hurt anything. I kind of thought they might."

"They took Juan back to the Devil's Hole," said Braddock.

Señora Belmosa knuckled tears away from her eyes and was able to say, "They . . . they left all the animals and said we could take them with us."

"Take them with you where?" Rojas asked.

"Wherever we go," the middle-aged woman replied with a pitiful note of despair in her voice. "They said that when they come back tomorrow, we should be gone, or else they . . . they would do other things . . ."

Braddock lifted a hand to stop her. They didn't need details of whatever depravities the outlaws had threatened to carry out against the Belmosa family.

"We're going to go find your husband," he said. "I reckon there's a good chance they just wanted to throw a scare into him, like they did with you."

Señora Belmosa shook her head. "No. I appreciate

what you are trying to do, señor Braddock, but I . . . I do not believe . . ."

"We'll find him and bring him back," Braddock said again. "Come on, Francisco."

They left the house and went to the shed, where Rojas got Juan Belmosa's saddle and put it on the farmer's horse. The gelding was old and stolid, but a good enough saddle mount for Belmosa's purposes. It would have to do for Rojas now, too.

As they rode up to the Devil's Hole a short time later, Braddock looked for any sign of Juan Belmosa. He didn't see the man anywhere.

"No rope tied onto a rock this time," Rojas observed grimly.

"Nope."

Braddock dismounted and walked up the slight incline. Rojas came with him. Braddock didn't hesitate as they approached the edge. Whatever was down there, dragging his feet wouldn't change it.

"Madre de Dios," Rojas said in a heartfelt whisper as the two men stood at the brink and peered down the dark shaft. Shadows were thick at the bottom, but they were able to make out the shape of a man floating face-down in the water that had collected there.

After a moment, Braddock sighed and shook his head. "We promised we'd bring him back," he said. "Reckon we'd better figure out a way to keep that promise."

———

BRADDOCK CARRIED a coiled rope on the dun, but it wasn't long enough to reach all the way to the bottom of the hole. He was pretty sure of that, but he got it from the saddle and let it down all the way to make certain. The end of the rope fell a good fifty feet short.

"Juan probably had some rope," Rojas said. "We can go back and look."

"You do that, if you will. I'm going to stay here and keep an eye on things."

Rojas hesitated and then said, "He's not going anywhere, G.W., and there's nothing you can do for him now."

"Maybe not, but I don't like the idea of riding off and leaving him alone."

Rojas shrugged and nodded. "Fine. I'll be back in a little while."

He rode off toward the farmhouse. Braddock walked around the Devil's Hole, thinking. Several ideas were stirring in his brain, but he couldn't put his finger on any of them.

The most important thing to remember, he told himself, was that the gang was escalating its activities and turning to murder and outright terror to accomplish its ends, which seemed to be to drive everyone from the Rio Grande Valley. He thought about Don Abraham Ordóñez and how the old man wouldn't be able to hang on to Rancho del Halcon if he suffered any more setbacks. The same was true of the other ranchers along the river. Make it difficult enough for them and they would have no choice but to leave, even though it meant abandoning land that had been in their families sometimes for generations.

From what Francisco Rojas had told him, the young man's father might be facing the same problem on this side of the border. He wouldn't be the only one, either. When a land truly became lawless, the law-abiding either wouldn't or couldn't remain.

Which would leave the valley wide open for whoever wanted to come in and seize it.

Braddock wasn't sure why anybody would go to that much trouble. The land along the river wasn't terrible range for ranching, but it was far from prime. It took a lot of that brushy country to support a substantial number of cattle. It was fertile enough that a man who was willing to work hard could scratch out a decent living from farming, as Juan Belmosa had proven, but except for the area right along the river, which flooded from time to time, it was too arid to be extremely productive. The river itself wasn't navigable much past Brownsville for anything bigger than a rowboat, so shipping wasn't a consideration.

Braddock didn't understand it, but he was sure something had to be going on that he didn't know about yet. Maybe he could find more answers in Chapparal City, if he could ever manage to get there.

Rojas returned a short time later with not one rope but two he had found at the Belmosa farm. "They're short enough that we'll have to tie them together and then tie them to the end of your rope for you to get down there," he explained.

"Who said I was going? I reckon you weigh a little less than I do."

"Not enough to make much difference," said Rojas. "And this *was* your idea. You said we promised his wife and kids that we'd bring Juan back, but *you're* the one who made the promise, G.W., not me."

"You could actually ride off and leave him down there to rot, after he extended his hospitality to us?"

"In return for us saving his life," Rojas said. Then he frowned. "But I suppose we kind of let him down in the long run, didn't we?"

"We're up against something here that may be too big for just the two of us to take on."

"Where do you think we're going to get any help?"

"This is the sort of hornet's nest that the Texas Rangers are supposed to clean out," Braddock said.

Rojas made a face and shook his head. "Sorry. I've never been that impressed with the Rangers."

Braddock kept his face impassive as he said, "Let's get these ropes tied together. I'll go down and get him."

"Juan said that more people might have been thrown down there. What about them?"

"I expect they're just bones by now, and we wouldn't have any way of knowing who was who. They can rest where they are."

After the nerve-wracking day they'd already had, it didn't help matters for Braddock to lower himself into that deep shaft at the end of a tied-together rope, even though both he and Rojas had checked the knots to make sure they were secure. The other end of the rope was tied around the horn on the dun's saddle. Rojas backed the horse away from the hole until the rope was played out to almost its full length. Then Braddock wrapped it around his waist, got a firm grip, leaned back against it and reached down with one leg to plant his foot against the hole's dirt wall. Rojas led the dun forward at a slow enough pace that Braddock was able to walk backward down the wall.

The sun was nearly at its zenith, so plenty of light penetrated into the shaft. Braddock looked back over his shoulder pretty often to gauge how deep he was and how much farther he had to go. He could see Juan Belmosa's body clearly now. He sort of hoped that the outlaws had shot Belmosa before throwing him in, so he wouldn't have had to experience the terror of falling to his death. But Braddock had a hunch that hadn't been the case.

Those masked bastards would have wanted to listen to him scream all the way down.

The rope was long enough to reach the water. "Hold it!" Braddock called up to Rojas, who brought the dun to a stop. Braddock extended one leg and probed under the surface. He found the muddy bottom pretty easily. The water was only about three feet deep. He let himself drop the rest of the way.

"Come ahead a little and give me some slack."

He rolled Belmosa over. No wounds were visible. Hitting that shallow water and the bottom underneath it was what had killed him. Braddock looped the rope under the farmer's arms, knotted it, and called to Rojas to have the horse pull him up.

When Rojas dropped the rope back into the hole, Braddock repeated that with himself. When he had his feet back on solid ground at the top, he was glad to be out of that hole.

"The Devil's Hole is right," he muttered. He and Rojas lifted Belmosa's body and draped it over the saddle of the farmer's own horse, then set out to take him home.

16

A COUPLE OF HOURS LATER, THE TWO MEN WERE ON THEIR way to Chapparal City for the second time on this tragic day. It was early afternoon when they set out from the Belmosa farm, so Braddock figured it would be close to evening by the time they reached the settlement.

Rojas was riding Juan Belmosa's horse. He had offered to have it returned to the farm once they got to town, but señora Belmosa told him that wouldn't be necessary. She would have no need of it. That very day, she said, she would hitch the two mules to the family's wagon, load her children and whatever possessions they had onto the vehicle, and leave the farm for good. She had a sister in MacAllen, she explained, who would take them in.

That would also mean leaving behind the freshly dug grave where her husband now rested, but Braddock could understand why she felt compelled to do that. The farm held nothing but bitter memories for her now, and if she stayed, the situation might well get worse. Juan

Belmosa's murderers had promised to come back, after all.

"Francisco and I feel that we owe him a debt," Braddock had said to her before they left the farm. "We'll do everything we can to bring those men to justice."

"But why?" señora Belmosa had asked. "You are just men, not the law."

"Sometimes those who are just men have to stand up and do the right thing," Braddock had responded. He didn't bother explaining to her that in his eyes, he still *was* a representative of law and order.

He and Rojas had dug the grave, of course, had laid Juan Belmosa to rest under the solemn, red-rimmed eyes of his family, and then helped the señora hitch up the mules and load the wagon. Rojas had pressed some money on her in payment for the horse, considerably more than the animal was worth, but the señora took it gratefully. She would need the help in making a new start. Then they had all left the farm behind, heading in different directions.

"You were kind of free in promising that we'd avenge Juan's murder, G.W.," Rojas commented as they rode through the burned-out area from the blaze that morning. The ground and the layer of ashes covering it had cooled off enough that it was no longer dangerous. The horses' hooves stirred up tiny gray clouds of ash as they walked along. "You take a lot on yourself, don't you?"

"You said somebody needs to break up that gang and that nobody else seems to be trying to do that."

"Maybe not, but it's still not our responsibility."

Braddock looked over at his companion. "You said your father has a ranch on the Rio?"

"That's right."

"Have rustlers been hitting him, too?"

Rojas shrugged. "So I've heard. I haven't been home for quite a while."

"Maybe that's what brought you to these parts in the first place?" suggested Braddock. "You want to help him out, along with all the other rancheros on both sides of the border who are suffering?"

"I'm not exactly on good terms with my father, G.W."

"Because you're not going to that university anymore?"

Rojas shook his head and said, "I don't want to get into it. Let's just say that my father and I both had our reasons for being upset with each other and let it go at that, all right?"

"It's none of my business," Braddock said with a shrug.

"No, it's not."

"I was just curious whether or not I can count on you the next time trouble breaks out."

Anger flared in Rojas's dark eyes. He glared over at Braddock and said, "I haven't let you down so far, have I?"

"You haven't."

"I don't run out on something once I've started it. And like it or not, I suppose I've thrown in with you on this . . . quest . . . of yours. Satisfied now?"

Braddock smiled. "As a matter of fact, I am. I'll feel even better about things if we can dig up some answers in Chapparal City."

"What makes you think we will? The gang we're after could have its headquarters anywhere on either side of the river for seventy or eighty miles."

"That's true. But if you think about where it lies on a map, Chaparral City is kind of central to the whole area. You could reach anywhere the gang has struck in a couple of days' ride." Braddock frowned in thought. "There's a town on the other side of the border called Los Pinos."

"I've heard of it," Rojas said.

"You could draw a pretty straight line from Chaparral City to Los Pinos," Braddock went on. "They're both in about the same position respective to the border, and in the center of the area where the gang has been operating."

"Now you're saying this other place is their head-quarters?"

"One of them, maybe."

Rojas frowned and shook his head. "So, you're back to thinking it's *two* gangs of raiders?"

"One gang, two parts," said Braddock. "An army is broken up into different companies, isn't it?"

Rojas rubbed his chin as if he were thinking. "Maybe a commander in each town, and some bigger boss over both of them?"

"It could work that way."

"But that's pure speculation on your part."

"Yeah, it is," Braddock admitted. "That's why I'm hoping we'll find some answers in Chapparal City."

"Only one way to find out, I suppose."

The two men rode on through the afternoon, keeping an eye out for more trouble.

———

THEY DIDN'T ENCOUNTER ANY, and by late afternoon, they came in sight of Chapparal City. There were some good-sized brick buildings lining both sides of a main street that stretched for several blocks, as well as side streets sprawling around where residences and a few smaller businesses were located.

The way things had worked out, neither man had had much of an appetite at midday, so they had skipped the noon meal. By now, however, their bellies were insisting on attention. Braddock nodded toward a building constructed of irregular blocks of rust-colored sandstone with a red tiled roof. An awning overhung a small, short porch in front of the place. On the front of that awning was a sign that proclaimed *RED TOP CAFÉ – GOOD EATS.*

"How about we stop there first?" Braddock suggested.

"That sounds like a fine idea," Rojas agreed. "My stomach thinks my throat has been cut, as you Americans say."

Braddock chuckled. It had been a grim day, but at least he and Rojas finally had reached their destination. And some mighty appetizing smells were drifting out through the Red Top's open door. Maybe that was a sign that their luck was going to turn.

Braddock wasn't going to count on that, though.

The hitch rail in front of the café was mostly full, but there was enough room for their horses. They stepped inside, saw an L-shaped counter to their left and tables covered with red-checked cloths to their right. The tables were all occupied; the Red Top obviously did good business. Several stools at the counter were empty, though, so Braddock and Rojas took a couple of them.

Rojas glanced around and said quietly, "There don't appear to be many of my people here."

"Maybe, but you're not the only *Tejano.* I don't expect we'll run into trouble."

Braddock wasn't so sure about that when he noted the scowl on the face of the man approaching them on the other side of the counter. The man was short and very stocky, with a fringe of grizzled hair around an otherwise bald head and a close-cropped beard. He wore a canvas apron over denim trousers and a shirt with the sleeves rolled up over hairy, muscular forearms. The apron might have been white once, but now it was gray.

"What do you boys want?" the man asked in a deep, rumbling voice.

"What's the best thing you have?" Braddock said.

"Steak fried good an' tough, like boot leather, and fried taters swimmin' in grease." The man laughed, and a sudden grin transformed his face. "I don't believe in pullin' no punches. But the food tastes better'n it sounds."

"We'll give it a try, then," said Braddock. "Two plates, and stack 'em high."

"Are you sure about this?" asked Rojas.

"Just wait and see," Braddock told him.

The counterman started to turn away but added over his shoulder, "Oh, there's apple pie, too. You'll want some o' that."

"Damn right," Braddock said.

Rojas still looked doubtful as the counterman yelled, "Two regular, and heap 'em!" through a window in the wall. Part of the kitchen was visible on the other side.

A man at one of the tables yelled, "Hey, Packy! Need another steak over here!"

"Hold your horses," the counterman told him. "Or that's what you'll be eatin' if you rush me! Horse meat!"

Braddock grinned at Rojas and asked, "Not what you're used to?"

"No, not really, but I'll reserve judgment, I suppose."

"I've eaten in plenty of places like this," Braddock assured him. "They may not look like much, but the food's usually good."

"One can only hope."

While they were waiting for their steaks, Braddock took the opportunity to look around the room at the other customers. He didn't expect to see anyone he recognized—but he hadn't expected to run across Ed Montayne back in Los Pinos, either.

As Rojas had noted, only a few other *Tejanos* were in the Red Top, and they were all sitting together at a large table toward the back of the room. Judging by the range clothes they wore, all of them were working vaqueros. Braddock figured they probably had riding jobs on one of the ranches in these parts.

Most of the other customers appeared to be Texas cowboys. A few men in town clothes sat here and there, but their outfits were overalls and rough shirts, not fancy duds like storekeepers or clerks might wear. This was a working man's café. Braddock didn't see any women in the place. As a result, the talk was loud and rather bawdy, punctuated by raucous laughter. A few of the men did cast side-eyed looks at Rojas, probably not because of his race but because his garments were the most expensive and colorful on display in the room.

The counterman, Packy, had gone through a swinging door into the kitchen. When he reappeared, he set two big plates in front of Braddock and Rojas. Each plate held a massive slab of beef accompanied by a small mountain of fried potatoes. As Rojas regarded the steak somewhat warily, Packy picked up a battered coffee pot from a stove behind the counter and filled two tin cups.

"Dig in," Braddock invited his companion. Rojas sighed and picked up the knife and fork Packy dropped beside his plate. He began sawing at the meat.

Despite what Packy had said earlier, the steak wasn't

as tough as boot leather. In fact, it was tender and juicy and very good. The potatoes, although they *were* a little on the greasy side, also had an excellent flavor. The coffee with which they washed down the food was strong and black, with no nonsense about it, just the way Braddock liked it.

"I must admit, this is better than I expected it to be," Rojas said a few minutes later between bites.

"I figured it would be good," Braddock said. "Places like this may not be fancy, but the folks who run them know how to feed a man."

Packy heard that comment and said, "You can thank my wife for that. She's the one back there in the kitchen cookin' up the grub."

"My compliments to her," Rojas said.

"Yeah, I'll pass that along," Packy said dryly. "You boys are new in town, ain't you?"

"Just rode in a little while ago," said Braddock. "This was the first place we stopped. We've been on the trail for a while, and we were hankering for a good meal."

Packy leaned on the counter and shook his head. "I hope you ain't hankerin' for work. There sure ain't much of that to be had around here."

"Why not?" Braddock asked in apparent ignorance.

Packy snorted. "You ain't heard? Some pack o' no-good bandits from across the border has been raisin' hell in these parts. They've hit the banks in half a dozen towns and have rustled so much stock from so many spreads, it don't hardly seem like there'd be enough room in Mexico for all them stolen beeves!" He shook his head. "The ranchers are hangin' on, but they can't take much more. And some folks in the towns are givin' up and movin' on, figurin' to try makin' new starts somewhere else. This is cattle country, and if the spreads go under, so does everything else."

Braddock frowned and asked, "Can't the law put a stop to it?"

"The law?" Packy repeated. "The county sheriffs and their deputies have been tryin', I suppose, but they're spread too thin, and that Mex outfit is too big and too well-organized. I heard that some of the ranchers have sent word to Austin, askin' for a company of Rangers to be sent down here, but nobody's seen hide nor hair of any such. It'd take a company at least to clean up that bunch. Maybe more."

Braddock couldn't say anything about it, but the pleas for help from the southern tip of Texas *had* drawn a response from Austin, in the form of John Edward Slattery, along with Slattery's recruitment of Braddock to lend him a hand. Braddock was sure Slattery had been trying to get a line on the man or men behind the campaign of terror along the border. If he had been successful, *then* he could have gotten word back to Austin and more Rangers would have been dispatched.

But now Slattery was dead and Braddock was on his own except for the young, college-educated *Tejano* dandy. Braddock remained convinced that Slattery's rendezvous with Ed Montayne meant Montayne was connected to the ringleaders. In the back of Braddock's brain was the thought that maybe he could infiltrate the gang where Slattery had failed.

Working against that was the fact that several of the outlaws had seen both him and Rojas. Trying to work their way into the bunch could mean signing their death warrants.

But if he *could* get the information he needed, a wire to Captain John Hughes would bring reinforcements.

Braddock was sure the cap'n wouldn't ignore a message from him, even if he was only an outlaw Ranger now, not the real thing.

Braddock tried not to let his mulling over of all that spoil his enjoyment of the meal. He said to Packy, "Well, even if we can't find any work, we still have a little bit of a stake, and it'd be nice to spend a night under a roof for a change. Is there a good hotel in town?"

"The Western Lodge," Packy replied. "A block and a half down on the left."

"How about a saloon where a man can get an honest drink, not some watered-down panther piss?"

"That'll be the Alhambra, other side of the street not far past the hotel."

Rojas said, "That's a rather elegant name for a . . . well . . ."

Packy laughed. "A saloon in a South Texas cattle town? You're right about that, mister. Fella who owns the place comes from Spain, or so he claims."

"I look forward to talking with him," Rojas murmured.

Packy waved a short, stubby finger at their empty plates. "Want another steak?"

"Good Lord, no," said Rojas. "I couldn't eat another bite."

"I reckon I'm done, too," Braddock said.

"All right, then," Packy said with a nod. "Time for pie. You hadn't forgot about that, had you?"

Rojas just groaned but waved for him to bring it on.

17

BRADDOCK AND ROJAS MANAGED TO GET DOWN BOWLS OF deep dish apple pie with cream ladled on top. As they left the Red Top, after Braddock had paid for their meals, Rojas groaned, rubbed his belly, and said, "I may never eat another meal. I can't imagine being hungry ever again."

"Food like that will stick to your ribs, all right," said Braddock, "but I expect you'll be hungry again by morning. Packy said his wife cooks up the best flapjacks in this part of the country, remember?"

"I could hardly forget. I suppose we can try them . . . if we live that long."

"You didn't eat so much that it's gonna kill you."

"I was thinking more of other dangers we might encounter," said Rojas. "We *are* looking for trouble, aren't we?"

"I reckon we are."

They untied their horses' reins and led the animals along the street. Braddock hadn't asked Packy about a good stable, but he spotted one with the name *PATTER-SON'S LIVERY* on a sign next to the double doors. He liked the looks of the place and gestured to Rojas that they should take their horses there.

The proprietor, a sturdily built man with graying red hair, frowned when he saw Rojas's horse. "That animal belongs to Juan Belmosa, don't it?" he asked. "I got a good memory for such things."

"I purchased it from señora Belmosa," Rojas explained. "Her husband passed away, unfortunately, and she no longer had need of the horse."

The liveryman's eyes widened in surprise. "Belmosa's dead, you say? What in blazes happened?"

Braddock felt an instinctive liking and trust for this man, so he went along with his gut and gave him a truthful answer. "A gang of owlhoots with masks on their faces killed him, according to the señora."

Patterson blew out an angry breath. "That bunch again! They've been making life miserable around here for months now. My business has suffered a lot, and plenty of others have had it even worse. As if they haven't done enough already, now the skunks have started murderin' innocent farmers?" The liveryman shook his head. "It's like they've declared war on every law-abidin' person along the border. From the rumors I've heard, the situation is almost as bad on the other side of the Rio Grande."

"It is," Rojas said, then added, "From what *I've* heard."

"I'm sorry for what I was thinkin', mister," Patterson said. "I was about to accuse you of stealin' Juan's horse, but I reckon it's a lot more likely what you told me is true, knowing how those varmints have been operating around here. Anyway, you don't exactly *look* like a horse thief."

"Thank you . . . I think."

"We'd like to leave our horses here for a few days," Braddock said.

"Sure. You know how long you'll be in Chapparal City?"

Braddock shook his head. "Not really."

"Well, you can pay me for a couple of days. If you wind up staying as long as a week, the rate per night will be lower, but we can square that up then, if it happens."

"Sounds good."

Braddock didn't expect that he and Rojas would be in Chapparal City for that long. Either they would have turned up the information they were looking for before then, or else their mission here would have proven to be a failure and they would have moved on.

Or, he thought, they could be dead . . .

They stopped at the Western Lodge Hotel long enough to rent a pair of rooms for the next two nights. As they were leaving the hotel, Rojas said, "I don't know about you, G.W., but my funds are getting perilously low."

"Mine, too," said Braddock. "I can scrape together enough for a drink at the Alhambra, though. I want to have a look at the place."

"So do I." Rojas rubbed at his chin and went on, "I think I may know a way to improve our financial situation."

Braddock narrowed his eyes. "Does it involve cards?"

"I'm quite an excellent poker player, you know."

"Well . . . I suppose it couldn't hurt anything. For one thing, you don't have much to lose."

"I certainly appreciate that vote of confidence," Rojas said. "Come along."

They saw the Alhambra, farther along the street. It

would have been difficult to miss. Light spilled through large windows on both sides of the entrance, which was situated on the corner of a block where one of the side streets intersected the main street. Large signs with the saloon's name on them were mounted on both walls above the boardwalk awning. The tinkling notes of piano music came from inside. Many of the businesses in Chapparal City might be having trouble making ends meet, but the Alhambra didn't appear to be one of them, Braddock thought as they approached and he took note of the crowded hitch rails on both streets fronting the place.

Of course, some men would always be able to find the price of a drink or a card game, even if they were struggling to survive in all other respects. Some even chose their own vices over supporting their families . . .

He wasn't here to worry about that, he reminded himself. Human nature was a bigger problem than he could ever solve. He was after the ringleaders of the outlaw gang stalking the border.

The interior of the Alhambra was smoky and noisy, smelled of beer, whiskey, and unwashed human flesh . . . just like hundreds of other saloons Braddock had been in over the years. The trappings here were nicer than some, however. Oil lamps in crystal chandeliers spread their light over the scene. The brass rail along the foot of the bar gleamed, as did its mahogany surface. Paintings of castles and pastoral landscapes adorned some of the walls, although the traditional portrait of an opulently endowed nude woman surrounded by equally naked cherubs hung behind the bar, flanked by long mirrors.

The bartenders—there were three of them—wore green vests over white shirts with red sleeve garters. Each man sported a black string tie, as well, and had his hair slicked down with pomade. They moved efficiently along the hardwood, dispensing drinks to the customers at the bar as well as filling trays with glasses to be delivered to the tables by attractive young women in short, low-cut, spangled dresses.

"Elegance and garishness in equal measure," murmured Rojas. "I suppose that's better than all garishness."

Braddock pointed toward an opening at the bar. "Let's have a beer."

The bartender who came up to serve them had a round, friendly face and a narrow mustache. "What'll it be, gents?" he asked with a smile.

"Is the beer cold?" asked Braddock.

"Well, now, would we serve anything less than that in the Alhambra? I don't think so, gents! We have an ice house in Chapparal City, and the boss makes sure we serve the coldest beer you'll find this side of San Antonio . . . and it's better than the suds you'll get there, too."

"Draw a couple for us, then," Braddock told him. He slid a coin across the bar. "And keep them coming until we've used that up."

The bartender looked a little askance at the silver dollar. "That'll be one apiece," he commented.

"Four bits for a beer? It better be cold."

The bartender filled two mugs and placed them in front of Braddock and Rojas. Braddock picked up his, took a long swallow, and licked foam off his upper lip.

"You weren't just bragging," he said to the bartender. "That's good."

"The boss won't settle for anything less."

Rojas said, "Who is this boss of yours? I believe someone told me that he's Spanish?"

"That's right. From Granada." The bartender nodded

toward a man standing in front of the far end of the bar, talking to several other men. "Señor Alcazar."

The saloon's owner was a tall, well-built, middle-aged man with graying dark hair. He wore an expensive gray tweed suit, and a diamond stickpin glittered in the center of his silk cravat. A thin black cigar rested between two of the fingers on his left hand. He puffed on it, exhaled a cloud of smoke, and laughed at something one of the other men had to say.

Some men got up from a nearby table and moved off. Braddock gestured with his mug toward the now-free table and said to Rojas, "Why don't we sit down?"

"All right."

They took seats and sipped their beers. Braddock tipped his head in a minuscule nod toward Alcazar and asked Rojas, "What do you think of him?"

"How in the world should I know anything about him?"

"Do you think he's a real Spaniard, or is that just an act he's putting on?"

Without being too obvious about it, Rojas studied Alcazar for a moment, then said, "Actually, I believe he's Moorish. Alcazar is derived from a Moorish name, and the Alhambra, well, that was a Moorish palace built on the ruins of some old fortifications from Roman times."

"The Moors are the folks who came over from northern Africa and conquered Spain for a while, isn't that right?"

"Yes. They called it al-Andalus. Some people think of them simply as black, but of course their heritage actually is much more complex than that, especially when it's been filtered through numerous generations of previously pure Spanish blood. In time, they went from conquerors to being looked down upon." Rojas drank some of his beer, then added, "Of course, the pure-bred Spanish think of the Mexican people the same way. Mutts and mongrels, that's what we are to them. And the *Tejanos* are even worse, because we choose to live in Texas."

"I've always thought mutts and mongrels are usually the best dogs you can find," Braddock said.

"And now *you're* comparing us to dogs."

"You ought to take it as a compliment. Dogs have purer hearts and souls than nearly all the human beings I've met in my life."

"Well, I won't get into that philosophical discussion with you." Rojas looked around and leaned forward in his chair as a man stood up at one of the tables where a poker game was going on. "I believe I see an open seat in that game."

"Are you sure about this?" asked Braddock.

"I'm certain."

Rojas drained the last of his beer and stood. He moved to the other table before anyone else could get there and rested his hand on the back of the empty chair.

"May I join you, gentlemen?"

A frock-coated gent who had the look of a house gambler was shuffling the deck. He glanced up and said, "You can if you have twenty dollars to buy in."

"As a matter of fact, I do."

Rojas dropped a gold double eagle on the table, and the dealer pushed some chips toward him. Rojas gathered them in and sat down.

Braddock wondered if that double eagle was the last coin the young man had to his name. He wouldn't be surprised if that were the case.

Braddock's gaze roamed around the table. In addition to the house gambler, four other players were in this game. Two were middle-aged townsmen with the look of merchants about them. Successful merchants, maybe, before outlaws and rustlers had begun ravaging the Rio Grande valley. Another middle-aged man was dressed in well-kept range clothes. A ranch owner, more than likely, Braddock decided. The fourth man also wore range clothes but was much younger. A cowboy who rode for one of the spreads in the area. Rojas was the only one at the table of Mexican descent, but none of the others had seemed to take offense when he asked to join the game, so Braddock figured they didn't care about that.

The dealer flicked cards around the table and the hand began. Braddock nursed the beer and watched from where he was, lounging at the other table with his legs stretched out underneath it.

The game seemed to be a friendly one, with some talk going around the table, although for the most part the players concentrated on their cards. Rojas bet carefully, lost a couple of hands but with minimal damage, then won a decent pot and almost doubled his money. After a few more hands had passed, he had more than doubled what he'd sat down with.

Braddock thought it might be a good time to cash in and go, but Rojas continued playing. He seemed to be enjoying himself, talking more now to the other players. Over the music of the piano in the corner and the hubbub of conversation in the saloon, Braddock couldn't hear what Rojas was saying, but he saw the young cowboy sitting to Rojas's right starting to look a mite annoyed.

That look of annoyance got even more pronounced

when the current hand ended and a grinning Rojas threw down his cards with a triumphant flourish, then leaned forward to rake in the pot.

The young cowboy reached out and slapped his left hand down on top of both of Rojas's hands, pinning them to the table with the pile of chips underneath them. The puncher said, loudly and clearly enough for Braddock to hear, "Hold on there a minute, *amigo.*"

The emphasis he put on the last word made it clear that he didn't consider Rojas a friend at all.

The three older men around the table frowned in disapproval. The house gambler leaned forward and said something to the cowboy. He wouldn't want gunplay erupting at his table. Blood being spilled on the green felt was bad for business.

Most of the other customers in the saloon hadn't noticed the confrontation, but a few at nearby tables had, and as they quieted down, a small bubble of silence formed in the middle of the noisy room. Braddock was on the outer edge of that bubble but close enough to hear the cowboy say, "Your luck sure has turned these last few hands, hasn't it, *amigo?*"

"Good fortune has a way of coming to those who are patient," said Rojas. "I hope you're not implying something more."

"I'm implyin' that your luck is a hell of a lot better when you're dealin' the cards!"

The house man said, "Take it easy, Carl. Rojas's game is on the up and up. You think I don't watch what goes on at my table? I'm always on the lookout for tinhorns and sharpers."

"Shut up, Hannigan. You're a tinhorn yourself. Probably in on it with this greaser."

"I thought I was your amigo," Rojas said, "and now

you call me names." His voice hardened. "Please, remove your hand from mine."

"No, sir. I ain't lettin' you take that pot. You better admit there's somethin' funny been goin' on, otherwise we're gonna have trouble, you and me."

"I believe we already do."

Over at the bar, Alcazar had finally noticed what was going on. His hawk-like face was turned toward the poker table, and he had straightened from his casual pose as he watched. The cigar was in his mouth, clamped between his teeth as his jaw firmed.

Braddock had already spotted a couple of burly hombres he figured for bouncers. He could tell that Alcazar was thinking about signaling for them to go over and break up the confrontation.

Braddock had considered doing the same thing himself, but he didn't want to draw attention. It was easier, usually, to find out what was going on in a town if folks didn't really notice him. But he wasn't going to just sit here and let anything happen to Rojas if he could prevent it. He tensed, ready to make a play as he saw the cowboy's other hand start drifting toward the gun on his hip . . .

Then the batwings at the saloon's entrance swung open and several men walked in. Braddock's eyes flicked in that direction and he drew in a sharp breath as he recognized the man in the forefront of that group. The last time Braddock had seen him had been on the other side of the border, in the stable at Los Pinos.

Ed Montayne had just walked into the Alhambra.

And even worse, Braddock realized with a shock, the men with him were the same ones who had thrown Juan Belmosa into the Devil's Hole with the rope tied around his ankle.

The same men, Braddock was convinced, who had murdered Belmosa earlier today . . .

18

Braddock had sat up straighter when the trouble started between Rojas and the young puncher. Now he slumped back in his chair again and tipped his head forward so that the brim of his hat partially obscured his face. Those killers had gotten good looks at both him and Rojas the day before, during the showdown at the Devil's Hole. They were liable to recognize Braddock now if they paid much attention to him, so he was going to try to avoid that.

Rojas had his back to them, so, for the moment anyway, he was safe from being identified. Braddock knew that probably wouldn't last long.

Montayne and his companions didn't seem to have noticed the tension in the saloon. They walked straight to the bar and leaned on the hardwood. Several customers moved aside to give them room. Montayne looked along the bar and nodded to Alcazar, who gave him a curt nod in return.

That didn't have to mean anything, thought Braddock as he observed the exchange. Montayne probably knew that Alcazar owned the Alhambra. It was common enough to greet the proprietor of a place when you came in to have a drink. That might be all it was.

But it might be more than that, too, and the possibility greatly intrigued Braddock. As the owner of the biggest and most popular saloon in Chapparal City, Alcazar had all kinds of men passing through here, all the time. It would be easy for the unmasked outlaws to blend in, especially the Americans. A lot of folks thought Mexican bandits were responsible for the trouble, but Braddock knew that wasn't the case. Not completely, anyway.

Those thoughts flashed through Braddock's mind in a couple of heartbeats. Meanwhile, the trouble brewing between Rojas and the young cowboy was still on the verge of boiling over into gunplay.

"I'm not going to confess to cheating when I've done nothing of the sort," Rojas went on. "You were simply outplayed, señor, and if *you* can admit *that*, we can continue to have a friendly game—"

"I don't want to be friends with a dirty, cheatin' greaser like you!" The cowboy jerked his gun from its holster as he yelled.

He was leaning forward over the table, and so was Rojas. That put their heads fairly close together. Rojas lunged and slammed the top of his head into the cowboy's face before the young man could swing the gun up. The blow knocked him backward in his chair and freed Rojas's hands.

Rojas surged out of his chair, clamped the fingers of his left hand around the wrist of the cowboy's gun hand, and pinned it to the table. At the same time, Rojas's other hand darted under his jacket and brought out a knife. He pressed the point against the throat of the squirming cowboy, who abruptly froze at the touch of cold steel.

The sudden outbreak of violence had drawn the attention of everyone in the room. A hush settled over the place. Braddock clearly heard Rojas say, "I repeat, I've done no cheating, but in the interests of peace, I'm willing to declare this hand null and void. Everyone can take back out what they put in. Will that satisfy you?"

"Wait a minute," the house gambler said. "That's not fair to you, mister. You won fair and square, as far as I could see. And if you hadn't, I would have called you on it myself."

"True enough," Rojas conceded, "but again, I want no trouble. And holding a knife still like this is rather difficult. I would hate for my hand to start shaking—"

"All right!" the cowboy said, being careful to move his throat as little as possible. "You ain't no cheat!"

"And about the other name-calling?"

"I . . . I'm sorry, mister. I apologize."

"Very well." Rojas took the knife away from the cowboy's throat and looked around the table. "The offer stands, gentlemen. You can reclaim your money that went into that pot."

"Nothing doing," said the cattleman. "Like Hannigan said, you won fair and square, son."

"Yeah," one of the merchants agreed. "Take it, it's yours."

The cowboy swallowed hard. He had one tiny drop of blood visible on his throat where Rojas's knife had penetrated the skin. He nodded and said, "I'd be obliged if you'd just take the pot, mister."

"In that case . . ." Rojas let go of the cowboy's wrist and used that hand to sweep the chips in front of him. "I believe I'll cash in for the evening."

"Reckon that's probably a good idea," Hannigan, the house gambler, muttered.

Braddock still hadn't moved from his chair. He'd been dividing his attention between Rojas and Montayne and the other outlaws. As best Braddock could recall, Montayne had caught only a hurried glimpse of him, in bad light, back in Los Pinos. It was unlikely the man would recognize him.

The same wasn't true of the four men with Montayne tonight. But their attention, like that of everyone else in the place, was focused on what was happening at the poker table.

And Braddock could tell by the way the men stiffened and stared that they recognized Rojas. One of them —the man who'd done most of the talking at the Devil's Hole—leaned forward and spoke quietly to Montayne, who looked at Rojas with a new interest.

Well, hell, thought Braddock.

But they didn't seem to have noticed him, so maybe he could salvage something from this situation after all. He waited while Rojas cashed in and stuffed the bills and coins the house man gave him into his pockets. Then Rojas swung toward the table where he'd been sitting with Braddock earlier.

Braddock gave his head the tiniest shake possible, hoping that Rojas would see it and understand. Then he leaned his head toward the bar.

Rojas was quick-witted; Braddock had to give him credit for that. Without the slightest hitch in his movement, Rojas continued turning until he was facing the bar. The whole thing looked entirely natural.

Unfortunately, it ended with Rojas and the outlaws, including Montayne, looking directly at each other.

Rojas just smiled coolly, ignored the men at the bar,

175

and started toward the saloon's entrance. Braddock knew that Rojas was trying to pull them away from him. The young *Tejano* was painting a huge target on his back. Braddock didn't want Rojas doing that for him . . . but if he drew the outlaws' attention to him now, then Rojas's effort would be for nothing and they would both wind up in deep trouble.

As long as Braddock remained on the loose, he might be able to help Rojas, as well as getting closer to the man they were really after.

He had to take the chance.

Montayne and the other men were talking hurriedly in low tones as Rojas left the Alhambra. Two of them nodded and went after Rojas. Montayne and the other two stayed at the bar.

Were they going to ambush Rojas? Cut him down in a hail of gunfire from the dark mouth of an alley? That seemed like all too real a possibility to Braddock. He couldn't stay here. Even though he knew it risked attracting attention, he stood up and walked unhurriedly toward the batwings. He pushed them aside and stepped out onto the boardwalk.

As he did, he glanced back and saw that Montayne had moved along the bar and now stood at the far end, talking with Alcazar. That wasn't proof of anything, but it was an indication that the saloon owner might well be tied in with the gang, if not, in fact, its ringleader.

Braddock put that out of his thoughts for the moment. He looked along the street, trying to see if he could spot Rojas and the two outlaws who had followed him out of the Alhambra.

Rojas had had time to cross the street diagonally and reach the hotel. Braddock didn't see him in that direction. He swung his gaze down toward the livery stable and the Red Top Café.

There was Rojas in his pearl gray sombrero, ambling along the same side of the street where Braddock stood. The high-crowned hat was unmistakable. Rojas's casual pace was that of a man who didn't have a care in the world.

Coming up behind him were the two outlaws who had followed him out of the Alhambra. Braddock trailed them quickly, his long-legged strides carrying him along the boardwalk and then down the shallow step at the end of it. He moved as quietly as possible so the two men wouldn't hear him following them, as they were following Rojas.

The shadows were thick in places. In others, light slanted from windows and doorways on both sides of the street. Rojas passed in and out of those oblongs of illumination, as did the men stalking him. Braddock took advantage of all the gloom he could find, in case either of the outlaws happened to glance back, but they seemed to have all their attention focused on Rojas. If they drew their guns, Braddock intended to cut loose on them, even though it would mean shooting them in the back. He'd rather do that than allow them to gun down his new-found friend.

They didn't pull their irons, though. Instead, as Rojas passed the mouth of an alley, they suddenly rushed him. They had closed in quite a bit already, so their swift charge had them practically on top of Rojas before he could turn around. He tried to whirl and meet the threat, anyway, as they swarmed him.

The attack didn't catch Braddock by surprise; he'd expected the outlaws to try something, otherwise why follow Rojas from the saloon? But even though he reacted instantly, he was still too far away to do anything before the men grabbed Rojas and hustled him into the alley.

As he approached the dark opening, he heard the frenzied shuffling of booted feet in the dirt, grunts of effort, and meaty thuds as flesh and bone struck flesh and bone.

"Hang on to him, damn it!" a man said in a low, urgent voice. "He's a slippery son of a bitch!"

"I got him!" said another man. "Use your gun on him! Buffalo the bastard!"

Braddock knew they were about to pistol-whip Rojas. Such an assault could be fatal. Even if they didn't stove in Rojas's skull, they were liable to injure him badly. He plunged into the alley, glad that his eyes had had a chance to adjust somewhat to the thick gloom.

He spotted the struggling figures in the shadows ahead of him. One of the outlaws had hold of Rojas from behind, arms wrapped around him tightly, while the other man pounded punches into Rojas's belly and face, alternating between the two. As Braddock catfooted up behind him, the outlaw paused and stepped back. He drew his gun and raised it, poised to come crashing down on Rojas's head.

Braddock picked up speed and cannonballed into the man from behind before the blow could descend. The impact knocked the man forward. He ran into Rojas and the other outlaw. Their legs tangled, and all three men went down.

Braddock would have fallen, too, if he hadn't been close enough to one of the buildings that he could slap his hand against the wall and catch his balance that way. He stepped back from the wildly flailing tangle of arms and legs and pulled his Colt, but in the dark, he couldn't tell who to hit. With his left hand, he fished a lucifer out of his shirt pocket and snapped it to life with his thumbnail, squinting his eyes against the sudden glare.

Braddock was ready for the light. The men on the ground in the alley weren't. They yelled in surprise and blinked, half-blinded. Braddock struck swiftly. The Colt rose and fell, thudding against an outlaw's skull and causing the man to crumple into a senseless heap.

The other outlaw had time to lash upward with a kick that caught Braddock's gun wrist. The Colt flew out of his hand as pain shot up his arm.

That was enough of a distraction for Rojas to writhe free of the man's grip. He hammered a fist into the outlaw's face, then struck again and again, getting some revenge for the beating the men had been giving him.

Braddock had dropped the match, too, when the man kicked him, but he had seen where his gun landed before the flame guttered out in the dirt. He stepped over to the spot, bent, and reached down. His fingers brushed the Colt's walnut grips and then closed around them. He straightened and brought the revolver up with him.

Rojas was still hitting the second outlaw. The thuds were soggy now, ugly sounds that told Braddock the man's face had been pounded into raw meat. He used his left hand to catch hold under Rojas's arm and tugged at the *Tejano*.

"He's out cold, amigo, if not worse," Braddock said. "You can stop hitting him now."

Rojas allowed Braddock to pull him to his feet. Braddock heard the young man breathing heavily, air rasping in his throat.

"This is one of the men . . . who threw Juan Belmosa in that damned hole," Rojas panted. "Who condemned the man's family to a life of poverty . . . Who's trying to ruin life for everyone in the valley . . ."

"I know," Braddock said, "but beating him to death and busting every bone in your hand while you're doing it won't bring Belmosa back, or help his family, for that matter."

"No, but every one of these men we dispose of is one less to carry out whatever it is they're planning."

"Maybe we ought to take these fellas somewhere and see if we can find out what that is."

Braddock figured he could get the men to talk. If they wanted to be stubborn about it, he could always turn them over to Rojas and see what results he could get—

"Down there!" a cry sounded from the alley mouth. "Kill them!"

Flame gushed from the muzzles of several guns, three or four at least, and a deafening peal of gun-thunder rolled along the narrow confines of the alley. Braddock grabbed Rojas and dived to the ground. Bullets scythed through the air, close above their heads.

Braddock's Colt was still in his hand. He returned the fire. There was no shortage of targets for him to aim at as he sprayed slugs toward the alley mouth. A man cried out, and the orange flashes splitting the darkness died away momentarily. Braddock figured the would-be killers had jumped for cover behind the buildings flanking the alley.

He and Rojas were still in a mighty bad spot, though, with nowhere to go to get out of it. He put his head close to Rojas's and said, "You roll right, I'll roll left. Stay close to the base of the wall and back away."

"They'll charge us any moment—"

"Just do it!"

Rojas grunted assent. Braddock rolled and came up

against the wall on his side of the alley. Lying on his belly, he started crawling backward. The other end of the alley was at least fifty feet away.

They would never make it. Braddock knew that. Maybe Rojas would stand a chance of getting away if Braddock reloaded his gun, sprang to his feet, and charged the outlaws. He could keep them busy while Rojas sprinted in the other direction. He stopped, felt in the loops on his shell belt for fresh cartridges, and working by feel with a deft touch honed by countless reloadings, thumbed them into the Colt's cylinder.

The night was eerily quiet now that the echoes had died away. A ways off, somebody yelled, wanting to know what the hell was going on. A dog barked. Then Rojas said, "G.W., when I open fire, you head for the other end of the alley as fast as you can."

What was the old saying about great minds working alike? Braddock said, "I was about to tell you the same thing—"

From the other end of the alley, behind them, a voice said, "Neither of you are going anywhere."

It was followed a series of ominous clicks that Braddock recognized as the sound of hammers being drawn back on several shotguns.

19

INTO THE QUIET THAT FOLLOWED THAT MENACING SOUND, Braddock said, "If you cut loose with scatterguns, your own men will wind up catching some of the buckshot."

"That'll be too bad for them," responded the voice that had spoken before. "They shouldn't have let the two of you nearly get away." In a brisk tone, the man went on, "I'm supposed to take the two of you alive if I can, but dead's just fine, too, if you don't give me any choice. So, stand up and throw your guns away, or we *will* open fire with these street sweepers. If they'll clean out a street, what do you reckon they'll do in a narrow alley like this?"

Braddock knew what they'd do. The loads of buckshot would rip him and Rojas to shreds. He'd heard at least three weapons being cocked. They could fire one barrel at a time and make sure nothing living remained in this alley.

"All right," he said as he climbed to his feet. "I'm tossing my gun your way."

"G.W.," Rojas said, "I don't know if this is the right thing to do."

"I don't see as we have any other choice."

Rojas sighed. "I suppose not."

Braddock threw his gun toward the back end of the alley and heard the thud when it landed. Rojas followed suit.

Whoever was giving the orders said, "I know you've got a knife, too, Mex. I saw it in the saloon when you threatened to cut that cowboy's throat. Toss it this way, too."

"Very well," said Rojas. Braddock heard steel clink against steel as the knife hit one of the guns when it landed.

"And you, mister, if you're carrying a blade, get rid of it."

"Just a clasp knife," Braddock replied. "Here it comes." He tossed it away. "I'm unarmed."

"As am I," Rojas added.

"You'd better be telling the truth." The man raised his voice. "All right, boys, grab them."

The men who had been shooting from the front end of the alley a few minutes earlier rushed along it, crowding around Braddock and Rojas in the shadows and wrapping them up in strong grips.

"All right, Ed, we've got 'em," a man called, confirming Braddock's hunch that Ed Montayne was running this part of the show.

"Hustle them this way," Montayne ordered. "We've already drawn too much attention."

With men gripping their arms tightly, Braddock and Rojas were forced along the alley. They emerged into the broad, open lane that ran behind the buildings. The light wasn't good back here, but it was a little brighter than in the alley. Braddock could see that he and Rojas were surrounded. Their captors all had shotguns or drawn handguns. The two prisoners were helpless, for the moment.

"Take them to the barn," Montayne said.

The outlaws hustled them along the back alley until they reached the rear of a big, somewhat dilapidated building. One of the men opened a door. The others shoved Braddock and Rojas inside. Darkness wrapped thickly around them until a man scratched a match to life and lit a lantern. The flickering glow revealed what appeared to be a deserted barn. Braddock heard a few scurrying sounds that had to be mice or rats, but there were no other animals in here.

Their captors dragged them over to an empty stall and threw them into it. Rojas lost his footing and fell, but Braddock managed to stay on his feet. He bent, hooked a hand under his friend's arm, and helped him up.

Both of them had lost their hats during the fight in the alley, but surprisingly, the outlaws had picked up Braddock's Stetson and Rojas's sombrero. They threw the headgear into the stall.

"There you go," Montayne said. "Might as well be properly dressed when you die."

Braddock picked up his hat, brushed it off, and put it on. "I think you've got us mixed up with two other fellas, friend," he said. "I never saw any of you boys before and don't know what it is you have against me."

Montayne laughed. "Next thing, you'll be sayin' that you don't know this Mex."

"I don't," Braddock said.

"Why'd you stick your nose in, then?" asked another man.

Braddock shrugged. "I saw him get jumped. Never did like it when somebody gangs up on a fella."

"He's lyin', Ed." That flat-voiced declaration came from the man who had led the bunch the day before. "Both of them were there at the Devil's Hole when we were tryin' to throw a scare into Belmosa. They're working together, all right."

"You weren't trying to throw a scare into him," Rojas said. "You threw *him* into the *hole.*"

"And that should've been enough to convince him to clear out," the outlaw barked back at him. "Instead, we had to go back there today and convince him permanent-like."

"After trying to kill us in that fire," Rojas said defiantly.

"I'm not surprised you two showed up here in town tonight," the outlaw said. "We knew you got out of that blaze somehow when you didn't find your bodies."

"Well, they won't get away again," said Montayne, sounding annoyed and impatient. "We'll make sure of that. But not until the boss has had a chance to talk to them." He grinned, but it wasn't a pleasant expression. "He wants some answers, and I reckon he's good at getting them."

Braddock didn't like the sound of that, but of course, that was exactly the reaction Montayne wanted to provoke. Braddock kept his face impassive. So did Rojas.

"I still say you've got this all wrong," Braddock said. "Sure, I got the drop on you boys yesterday. Seemed like a loco thing you were doing. Francisco came along just then and thought the same thing. But we'd never laid eyes on each other before, and that's the gospel truth."

It actually was, for all the good it would do them, thought Braddock.

"Then we rode on into town today," he continued. "But you seem to think we're working together, and we're not. I don't know what your game is, but it's none of our business. Let us go, and we'll walk out of here . . . hell, we'll ride out of Chapparal City tonight . . . and you'll never see us again."

"I don't think we'll ever see you again," Montayne said, "but it won't involve letting you go."

Braddock had figured that would be the outlaw's response. He had made the pitch anyway. Now that it hadn't worked, he could turn his thoughts to trying to come up with some other way of getting out of this fix.

Montayne turned to the other men. "Four of you stay here and keep an eye on them. I'll go let the boss know we grabbed them. The rest of you stay close, in case we need you later."

Four men, all armed with shotguns, remained in the abandoned barn. Two stood in front of the stall where Braddock and Rojas were and kept the Greeners pointed toward the ground but ready to swing up and blast if they needed to. The other two moved out of sight but didn't go far. Braddock could still hear them talking and chuckling to each other. Matches scraped as they rolled and lit quirlies.

Rojas looked at Braddock and said quietly, "Maybe we should have kept fighting."

"Then we would have *died* fighting. This way we can still accomplish something, if we get the chance. You heard Montayne. The boss wants to talk to us."

"Montayne?"

"That's right, you don't know him. He's that fair-haired fella who did most of the talking. Pretty well-known outlaw in some circles."

Rojas looked slyly at Braddock and said, "Some circles, eh? Ranger circles?"

Braddock recalled that Rojas didn't have too high an opinion of the Rangers. Maybe he had decided that being a Ranger would explain Braddock's determination to break up the gang wreaking havoc along the border. Braddock wasn't going to say anything either way about it, but if the outlaws searched him too thoroughly, they might find the badge in the hidden pocket on the back of his gunbelt. And if they did, he doubted if they would pause to ponder the meaning of the bullet hole through it. They'd just go ahead and put a .45 slug through his brain and be done with it.

Rojas didn't press him on the matter. Instead, he said, "Do you see any way out of here?"

Braddock glanced at the shotgun-wielding outlaws, who both were alert. "Not yet," he told Rojas under his breath. "But I'm not giving up, either."

A short time later, footsteps sounded from the front of the old barn. The guards raised their shotguns and backed off a little. Ed Montayne ordered from outside the stall, "You two come out here. If you're waiting for us to get in the line of fire, you're gonna have a long wait."

As a matter of fact, Braddock *had* been hoping for that. He and Rojas looked at each other. Rojas shrugged. He was right, Braddock thought. They didn't have much to lose.

They walked out of the stall as the guards kept the shotguns trained on them.

Montayne and several other men stood to the left. Braddock turned in that direction and wasn't surprised when he saw that one of the men was Alcazar, the owner of the Alhambra. Alcazar being here was the last "i" dotted and the last "t" crossed in his and Rojas's death warrant, Braddock knew. The saloonkeeper wouldn't have revealed his connection to the outlaws if he didn't expect that both of them would be dead soon.

Alcazar had donned a gray, soft felt hat upon leaving the saloon. He had another cigar in his mouth, which he puffed on meditatively as he looked at the two prisoners. After a moment, he took the cigar from his mouth and said, "Save yourself some pain and trouble, gentlemen. Tell me what you're doing here in Chapparal City and why you keep interfering in my business."

"You've got it all mixed up, mister," Braddock said. "Yeah, we poked our noses in where we shouldn't have, maybe, but that was a mistake. We were just trying to help out that poor farmer. We didn't know he was standing in the way of your plans."

Alcazar glared. "Do you know who I am?"

"Someone said you own the Alhambra," Rojas ventured.

"I'm Mauricio Alcazar. No one stands in the way of my plans, let alone some stupid farmer or a couple of saddle tramps." Alcazar turned his glare toward Montayne. "Do you really think a pair of nobodies like this represent an actual threat to our operation? Just look at them!"

Anger flashed in Montayne's eyes, but he kept a tight rein on his temper. He pointed at Braddock and said, "This is the one I was mostly worried about. He was in Los Pinos two nights ago, and he was at the Rancho del Halcon the night before that. Seems kind of funny he keeps turning up in places where he shouldn't."

Alcazar frowned. "What was he doing in Los Pinos?"

"Lurking outside the stable where I was talking to that fella who wanted to throw in with us."

"The one you had to kill when he tried to stop you from going to our associate's aid?"

"That's right. He said his name was Edwards and that you'd sent him to talk to me—"

"And I told you that I know nothing about that," Alcazar interrupted. "That was just a ruse. That man Edwards, I'm convinced he was a lawman of some sort. Probably a Texas Ranger." He looked at Braddock. "And this man might be, too, I suppose." He tossed the cigar butt at his feet and ground it out with a toe of a boot buffed to a high shine. "Search him."

"You reckon he'll have his badge on him?"

"Find out," Alcazar snapped.

Braddock stiffened. "I don't cotton to being manhandled," he said.

Ed Montayne drew his Colt and pointed it at him. "Well, that's just too damn bad—"

"G.W., look out!" Rojas said.

Braddock heard a noise behind him and realized that one of the guards had slipped around back there. He started to turn, but as he did, from the corner of his eye he saw the outlaw driving a shotgun butt at his head. The blow landed solidly, dropping Braddock into a darkness deeper than that grim hole in the ground miles northwest of here.

———

CONSCIOUSNESS SEEPED BACK into Braddock's head, which was a surprise in itself. If the outlaws had found his Ranger badge, they would have killed him then and there. Somehow, they must have overlooked it.

They had decided to keep him alive, maybe so they

could question him some more. Had they spared Rojas, too?

And why did the world keep rocking back and forth underneath him?

As a ball of sickness coalesced inside Braddock's guts, he slowly realized that he was draped over a saddle and lashed into place. A rope ran under the horse's belly from his wrists to his ankles. He tested the strength of the knots that held him and found them to be secure. Other than that, he tried not to move. If he shifted around too much, he might dislodge himself and slide around so that his head was hanging straight down. The position he was in was bad enough.

The horse carrying him plodded on. He heard hoof-beats around him from other horses, too, and could tell that he was in the middle of a group of riders. They weren't taking any chances with him, although as far as he could see, he was pretty much defenseless right now.

A groan tried to well up inside him, but he managed to hold it back, figuring it might be better for now not to let his captors know he was conscious again. He needed to find out where they were, and where they were going, before he could start trying to plan his next move.

The horse rocked along. Braddock wondered if it was his dun or some other mount. If it wasn't the dun, he hoped his trail partner was all right.

He slitted his eyes the tiniest amount, hoping to see something that would give him more information about his circumstances. Only blackness, faintly relieved by an occasional flicker of shadows, met his gaze, though. It was night, and the group was traveling through an area where there were no lights.

Braddock's head-down position finally took its toll,

causing his stomach to twist and spasm violently. He couldn't keep himself from retching.

"Hold it," a man ordered as Braddock emptied his belly. The order wasn't directed at Braddock, but rather at the men with him. "He's got to be awake after that," the man went on. "Get him down and tie him upright in the saddle. As sick as he is, I don't reckon he's much of a threat, but be careful, anyway."

The outlaw was right about that. Braddock felt so bad and was so weak he couldn't outfight a week-old kitten. As the spasms began to pass, he felt strong hands grip him. A knife cut the rope holding his arms and legs together. His captors dragged him off and let him fall to the ground . . . thankfully, not on the side of the horse where he'd just been sick.

They hauled him upright, stuck his foot in a stirrup, and lifted him into the saddle. A fresh length of rope was passed around his wrists, binding them to the saddle horn. They left his feet free. Somebody lifted a canteen to his lips so he could get a mouthful of water and rinse his mouth.

That was oddly considerate of them, he thought, since they probably planned to kill him before too much longer. But he supposed they figured there was no reason for him to be miserable until then.

"All right, let's go," the same man ordered. The riders who had dismounted to deal with Braddock got on their horses again, and the group started off.

Now that he was sitting up, Braddock was able to look around. No moon floated in the ebony sky, but enough light came from the millions of stars for him to make out the brush-covered countryside around him. They were following a trail through the chapparal. From the position of the stars, he guessed they were heading northwest, but he wasn't sure about that.

Three men rode ahead of him, three behind. And one beside him. Braddock had already figured out who that had to be. The man was slumped forward in the saddle, evidently conscious but not too aware of what was going on. Braddock said quietly, "Francisco."

The man stirred slightly, lifted his head. "G.W.?" he murmured. "You're . . . alive?"

Rojas's voice was thick and distorted. Braddock could see why. The young *Tejano*'s face was swollen and had dark smears on it. Blood from the beating he had received.

"We're both alive," Braddock said.

"For now," mumbled Rojas. "But I'm sure you can guess . . . where they're taking us."

Braddock had figured that out, too. He said, "To the Devil's Hole."

20

"THEY QUESTIONED ME AFTER THEY SEARCHED YOU," ROJAS said. He kept his voice low enough that only Braddock could hear it well enough to understand the words over the sound of the horses' hooves. "It was a rather vigorous interrogation, as you probably can guess."

"What did you tell them?" asked Braddock.

"The truth, as far as I know it. That you wanted to help the people who are being attacked on both sides of the border and that you persuaded me to go along with you. A rather foolish decision on my part, it appears now."

"They plan to throw us in the hole?"

"So that we'll disappear forever."

Braddock rocked along in silence for a moment, then asked, "They didn't find anything when they searched me?"

"Not that I'm aware of. Was there anything to find?" Rojas laughed softly. "Have you been keeping secrets from me, G.W.?"

"Never mind," Braddock said. He supposed he'd been

lucky and they had overlooked the hidden pocket in his belt. "You reckon we ought to make a break for it, try to lose them in the chaparral?"

"The men behind us are carrying shotguns. I expect they would blow us out of the saddle before we'd have a chance of getting away."

"I'm not going to let them throw me in that damned hole. Not while I'm still alive, anyway."

"Admirable determination. I'm not sure what we can do to prevent it, though."

"Let me think on it."

Braddock was riding his own horse. He had recognized the dun as soon as he was upright in the saddle again. It would respond to his commands, and he was willing to bet it could outrun any of the outlaws' mounts. But here in this damned brush country, there wasn't enough open space for a horse to build up much speed . . .

The landscape changed, became darker around them. The vegetation was sparser. Braddock didn't need the smell of ashes in his nostrils to know they had reached the area where flames had swept through the previous day, almost incinerating him and Rojas. That meant they weren't far from the now-abandoned Belmosa farm and the Devil's Hole a short distance beyond it.

Braddock heard a faint nervousness in Rojas's voice that he'd never heard before as the young *Tejano* said, "If we're going to do something, G.W., it will have to be soon."

"I know. Your hands are tied to the saddle horn, too, aren't they?"

"That's right."

The outlaws weren't leading the horses Braddock and Rojas rode. Surrounded the way they were, the mounts had gone along with the others without having to be led. Braddock was on the right, Rojas on the left, as they rode side by side. Braddock knew the dun would respond instantly to pressure from his knees.

"I'm going to make a jump to the right," he whispered. "That'll draw their fire after me. They'll turn their guns that way without even thinking about it. When I make that move, you go the other way. Don't even hesitate. Just light a shuck out of here, as fast as you can."

"While they shoot you down, you mean."

"Well, if that's the way it turns out, I'll be counting on you to settle the score for me, amigo. But first, one of us has to get away, get loose, and find some help."

"Who do you suggest? The Texas Rangers? I'm afraid it would take them too long to get here."

Braddock didn't say anything to that. "Just be ready when I make my move—"

The three outlaws ahead of them suddenly reined in. The leader turned his horse and demanded harshly, "What the hell's all the whispering back there? If you two are trying to cook up some trick—"

"Now!" Braddock shouted as he dug his knees into the dun's flanks and sent the big horse leaping to the right.

His prediction came true as the outlaws jerked their guns toward him and opened fire. Shotguns boomed as foot-long tongues of flame spouted from their muzzles. The dun leaped and cried out as buckshot stung its hide. Braddock was bent over as far as he could go in the saddle, hoping that would make him a small enough target. He felt something bite painfully into the back of his right shoulder, but other than that, he didn't seem to be hit. Or maybe he was mortally wounded and just in too much shock to know it.

Revolvers blasted behind him, too. He thought he heard slugs whine past his head, but that could have been his imagination.

"Damn it, the other one's getting away! Don't let him reach the chapparal!"

If Rojas could make it out of this burned region and back into the thick brush, he might stand a chance to giving his pursuers the slip. Braddock had to give him the best chance possible to do that.

With his hands tied to the horn, he couldn't rein in, but he could use his knees to prod the dun into a broad, sweeping turn. He swung around and pounded back toward them, yelling like a banshee. He wished his hands were free and he had a gun. He had never minded charging into the face of overwhelming odds. Sometimes a man could win through with sheer bravado. It was said of the Texas Rangers that they would charge hell with a bucket of water. Braddock had always tried to live up to that.

Tonight, the best he could do was distract his enemies while his ally tried to get away. Dark shapes on horseback loomed up in front of him. Orange muzzle flame stabbed through the shadows. Braddock felt the hot breath of bullets against his cheeks.

Suddenly the dun went down. Tied to the saddle horn as he was, Braddock couldn't leap clear. He came crashing down, too, although he managed to get his feet out of the stirrups so that momentum swung his body up and out. He landed so hard it jolted every bone in his body and drove all the air from his lungs, but at least the dun didn't roll on him. He lay there stunned, heartsick because he thought his old friend had been fatally wounded.

But then the dun neighed angrily and flailed its legs,

fighting to get up. Braddock forced his muscles to work and wrapped both hands around the horn. As the dun got its hooves under it and surged upright, Braddock came up, too, dragged by his grip on the saddle.

He never would have made it to his feet otherwise. He was too shaken.

Riders pounded up all around him. Starlight glittered on gun barrels. Braddock expected to feel the shock of multiple bullets striking him. Instead, the outlaws held their fire and he leaned his head against the saddle as his heart slugged wildly in his chest and he struggled to get enough breath back in his body.

"What the hell's . . . wrong with you boys?" he managed to say mockingly. "Why don't you . . . just go ahead and shoot me?"

A torrent of curses washed over him from the leader of this bunch. "Shooting's too damned good for you," he raged. "You're going in that hole. We're not going to just throw you in, either. We're gonna tie a rope around your feet, and then I'm going to take a knife and fray it. You'll have to hang there, not knowing how long it'll be before what's left of the rope snaps and drops you to your death. What do you think about that, mister?"

Braddock grinned up at the man, even though he didn't know if the outlaw could see the expression in the dark. "My friend must have gotten away, otherwise you wouldn't be so upset."

"Get him back on the damn horse!" The outlaw's anger confirmed that Rojas had escaped.

Braddock's captors closed in, dismounted, lifted him into the saddle again. When they started off, leading the dun this time, Braddock could tell the horse was limping a little. Evidently, the tumble had lamed the dun but not broken anything, and the wounds from the buckshot seemed to be minor, like the one in the back of Braddock's shoulder. Hurt like blazes, but it wouldn't kill him.

His captors had other ideas about that. But even though he dreaded what was waiting for him, he was glad that Rojas had gotten away. There was no sign of the young *Tejano* now.

But Rojas was alone . . . and what good could one man do against an outlaw horde?

———

THE GRAY GLOW in the eastern sky had lightened enough for Braddock to see fairly well around him by the time they reached the Devil's Hole. He was able to confirm that the dun wasn't injured too badly, although the horse needed rest if it wasn't going to be lamed permanently.

The leader of the six outlaws was the man who'd been in charge when Juan Belmosa was thrown into the hole. It seemed to Braddock as if more than two days had passed since that incident. Less than two full days, in fact. He felt as if he had known Francisco Rojas for a lot longer than that. But men bonded quickly when they fought side by side against steep odds.

They reined in a short distance outside the ring of boulders around the hole. The leader said, "Get him off his horse and bring me a rope."

"Sure, Dunlap," one of the other outlaws replied.

That was the first time Braddock had heard the man's name, he realized.

They cut him loose from the saddle horn, but as soon as his feet were on the ground, they lashed his wrists together again. Then they shoved him between a couple of the boulders to a spot near the hole's edge. A man brought over a coiled rope. Dunlap gestured at Braddock and ordered, "Tie one end around his ankles and the other around that rock over there, just like we did with Belmosa."

Once that was done and the knots were fastened securely, Dunlap sat on a rock and picked up the slack rope. He pulled a clasp knife from his pocket, opened it with his teeth, and started sawing on the rope. Strand after strand parted under the sharp blade until only a few remained intact.

"That ought to do it," he said. He stood up, closed the knife, and put it away. "You got anything to say, mister?"

"What could I say at this point to change anything?" asked Braddock coolly.

"Well, you might say you're sorry that you ever stuck your nose in our business where it doesn't belong."

"And if I do, you'll let me go?"

Dunlap threw his head back and laughed. "Not a chance in hell," he crowed.

"Then get on with it," Braddock snapped.

Badge or no badge, as far as he was concerned, he was going to die in the line of duty as a Texas Ranger. That was all he had ever expected out of life. When you got right down to it, that was all he had ever wanted, to be a member of the finest bunch of outlaw-hunters in the West, with all the dangers that went along with such an existence. And if his luck was about to play out, he could accept it.

He would have liked to go down fighting, though, with a six-gun in his hand as he dispensed lone star justice to these craven owlhoots—

"Throw him in!" Dunlap barked. The command was barely out of his mouth when, a split-second later, a shot blasted somewhere nearby and the outlaw leader's head jerked. Braddock felt a hot spray of blood in his face from the hole that suddenly opened up in Dunlap's forehead. The bullet that had just bored through the outlaw's brain narrowly missed Braddock's head.

The slug's impact knocked Dunlap forward. Braddock tried to get out of the way, but there wasn't enough time. As the other outlaws yelled alarmed curses and scrambled to draw their guns and hunt cover, Dunlap's body crashed into Braddock and knocked him backward, into the empty air above the Devil's Hole.

He plunged straight down, the frayed rope trailing from his ankles.

21

BRADDOCK WASN'T THE ONLY ONE TO FALL INTO THE Devil's Hole. Dunlap rolled over the edge, and his corpse plummeted toward the bottom, too.

Terror filled Braddock's brain, but a small part of it refused to give up, refused to stop working. Dunlap had wanted to torture him by letting him dangle until the frayed rope gave out, which meant the outlaw must have left enough of the strands intact that he thought they would support Braddock's weight for a while, even though the jerk of his weight hitting the end of the line would weaken it even more.

But if the dead weight of the falling corpse struck Braddock, more than likely that would be enough to break the rope right then and there. Braddock tried to twist his body and swing it to the side, praying that would be enough to make Dunlap miss him.

The sudden jolt as he stopped stabbed pain into Braddock's knees and hips, but the rope held and so did his joints. An instant later, he felt Dunlap's corpse brush past him. Fortune smiled on him. None of the dead outlaw's clothes caught on Braddock. A heavy splash came from below as the corpse struck the water in the bottom of the hole.

Up above, so many gunshots blasted that it sounded like a small-scale war was going on.

Braddock didn't know who had come to his aid, although he suspected that Rojas might have had something to do with it. But whoever was trying to help him, it would go for naught unless he could get out of here somehow. He figured the rope wouldn't hold his weight for more than a minute or two.

The gray circle of light at the top of the hole was tinged with streaks of gold and orange now. The sun was coming up. He forced his head and shoulders to bend so he could look at the rope. The frayed place was about two feet above his ankles. Maybe two and a half. If he jackknifed his body upward, could he reach that far and try to grab hold of the rope *above* the frayed spot? It would have been easier, he thought, if his wrists hadn't been tied together, but at least his hands were in front of him. If the outlaws had tied them behind his back, he would have had no chance at all.

He had to try, and there was no time to waste. Grunting with effort, he struggled to lift his torso toward his feet.

He raised his arms as much as he could but fell short. He could hold his body in that jackknifed position for only a short period of time before he had to drop back down and then try again. Blood pounded insanely in his head as he made another failed attempt to grasp the rope, then again and again. His pulse thundered so loudly that at first he didn't realize the shooting had stopped.

Reaching up again, he saw that more of the rope

strands had parted. Only a couple still held him up, and they were bound to break in a matter of seconds.

Something interrupted the light from the opening at the top of the hole. Braddock saw the silhouette of a man's head. Another rope writhed and fell toward him.

"Grab the lariat, G.W.!"

Braddock reached out, felt his fingers brush his only hope for salvation. It swung away from him. He heard a loud snap as the last two strands of the rope around his ankles parted. He grabbed desperately as he started falling. Both hands closed around what felt like a rawhide lariat. His body dropped, and he hung on for dear life.

This time it was his shoulders that took the strain as his weight hit them. He groaned from the strain, but his grip on the lariat didn't slip.

"Hang on, G.W., and we'll pull you out of there."

That was Rojas, all right, no doubt about it. Braddock had no idea who he'd found to help him, but they had gotten here in time and, for the moment, that was all that mattered.

The rope began to rise. Braddock clung to it, being lifted slowly out of the earth toward the growing daylight. Two more heads and sets of shoulders joined Rojas. As soon as Braddock came within reach, arms extended down and hands grasped his clothes, lifted him more, fastened securely under his arms. Safely in the grasp of his rescuers, he emerged from the Devil's Hole and sprawled face down on the ground as the men who had pulled him out rolled onto their backs on both sides of him.

Panting, he lifted his head and looked to his right at Francisco Rojas, who grinned back at him. Rojas's face was filthy with ash and dirt, and as Braddock looked at him, a shock of surprised recognition went through him.

Before he even had a chance to think about that, someone else loomed over him and a familiar voice asked, "Señor Braddock, are you all right?"

A woman's voice.

Braddock lifted his head and looked up into the beautiful face of Rosalita Ordóñez.

Seeing Rosalita here couldn't have come as a bigger surprise to Braddock. Once again, she was dressed for riding in tight black trousers and a black vest over a red silk shirt, as she had been the first time he'd laid eyes on her. She had tucked her raven hair under a flat-crowned black hat and strapped a gunbelt and holstered revolver around her trim hips.

During that first encounter, she'd tried to have him whipped. This time, it looked like she had helped save his life.

Several vaqueros from Rancho del Halcon stood around near the Devil's Hole. Rosalita gestured at them and commanded, "Help him up."

A couple of vaqueros hurried to obey the order, bending to grasp Braddock's arms and lift him to his feet. His head was spinning from being upside down so much these past few hours, but he dragged in a few deep breaths and began to feel better. Rojas stood, too, and clapped a hand on his uninjured shoulder.

"Are you all right, G.W.?"

"I've got a piece of buckshot in this other shoulder that stings a mite, but I reckon I'll live, thanks to señorita Ordóñez and her men. And thanks to you . . . Chuco."

Rojas winced. "Please. That name is very degrading. How long have you known?"

"A while," Braddock lied. He wasn't going to admit that he had just figured it out a few moments earlier, when he saw Rojas's face with as much grime on it as

204

had been there back in Los Pinos when he was pretending to be a ragged beggar. Braddock felt a little foolish for not seeing it sooner. In fact, he had referred to Rojas in both identities as an odd bird. Remembering that made him even more annoyed with himself. Rojas had done a good job in his masquerade, though.

Braddock went on, "Is your name really Francisco Rojas?"

"As a matter of fact, it is."

"Why were you pretending to be a beggar?"

Rosalita spoke up, saying, "You two can discuss this later." Braddock was grateful for her help, but she still displayed some of the haughty, imperious attitude she had demonstrated during their first meeting and later at the ranch headquarters. She went on, "I want to get back to Chapparal City and find my brother."

"Javier's in Chapparal City?"

"He was last night. I followed him there."

Braddock nodded slowly, putting more things together in his mind. "He was there meeting with his partner, I suppose."

"His partner?"

"Mauricio Alcazar."

Rojas said, "You believe young Ordóñez is working with Alcazar?"

"I believe they're the ringleaders of the bunch that's been raising hell along the border."

"You're insane," Rosalita said coldly. "That would mean he has been working against my father."

"You've been following him around," said Braddock. "That must mean *you're* suspicious of him, too. He trailed me to Los Pinos after I left your father's rancho, didn't he?"

Rosalita glared at him in the dawn light but didn't say

anything. That was answer enough, as far as Braddock was concerned.

"He was in that livery stable when Ed Montayne met with Slattery. He jumped me from the hayloft and tried to kill me."

Rojas said, "I'm guessing that Slattery was a Texas Ranger?"

Braddock nodded. "That's right. He was working undercover, trying to get on the inside of the gang and find out who's responsible for that campaign of terror."

"And he was your partner," Rojas said.

"Not exactly. What makes you say that?"

Rojas plucked something from the sash he wore and extended his hand. Braddock's Texas Ranger badge lay on his palm.

Braddock stiffened and said, "Where did you get that?"

"I found it in the pocket on the back of your gunbelt when I searched your belongings while we spent the night in Juan Belmosa's shed."

"You didn't have any right to go poking through my gear," Braddock snapped. He took the badge from Rojas.

"Perhaps not, but you interrupted me when I trying to find out more about you in your hotel room in Los Pinos." Rojas shrugged. "I'm curious, and I don't like to leave things unfinished."

Braddock glared for a second but then said, "All right. You did save my life a couple of times, here today and in that livery stable in Los Pinos, when you cut loose with that Winchester."

"You figured out that was me, too, eh?"

"I started wondering about it when I shot that javelina and you said we were even. At that point, Francisco Rojas hadn't saved my life . . . but Chuco had."

That was stretching the truth a little, too, but now that he looked back on it, Braddock could see how everything fit together. Not just Rojas pretending to be a filthy beggar, but other things, as well. The man who had attacked him in the alley behind the livery stable in Los Pinos had seemed to know who he was, and that meant he had to come from Rancho del Halcon. Javier Ordóñez fit that description, and he was used to giving orders.

That had been the second attempt on his life, Braddock recalled. Somebody had taken a shot at him in the garden of Don Abraham's hacienda. That could have been Javier, too.

"None of this makes sense to me," Rosalita said. Then, in a voice tinged with worry, she went on, "But Javier has been very different of late. Colder, more unfriendly. He has always been a very ambitious young man. And then, he began disappearing at times with no explanation . . ."

"Meeting with the gang working for him, I imagine," said Braddock.

Rosalita sighed. "My father never saw the change in him, but I did. And I thought something was wrong. That is why I began following him—" She drew in a sharp breath, as if something had just occurred to her. "That night in the garden of my father's house . . . could he have been shooting at *me?*"

"I don't know," Braddock replied honestly. "I suppose it's possible, if he wanted to get you out of the way so he'd be the only heir to Rancho del Halcon. We can ask him when we catch up to him."

"We're going after him?" Rojas said.

"If he's still in Chapparal City when we get there," Braddock said.

22

THE REST OF THE OUTLAWS HAD BEEN WIPED OUT WHEN Rojas, Rosalita, and the loyal vaqueros who accompanied her from Rancho del Halcon had opened fire from the brush. They left the bodies where they had fallen. The proper authorities could be notified later where to find the corpses . . . although for all practical purposes, it was likely the javelinas roaming the chapparal would have taken care of the problem by then.

Braddock couldn't bring himself to feel any sympathy for the varmints, not after they'd helped make life a living hell for folks along the border for months now.

Braddock had taken his shirt off long enough for Rojas to use the point of a vaquero's knife, disinfected with tequila, to dig that piece of buckshot out of his shoulder.

"Looks like it missed any bones," Rojas had commented as he cleaned the wound, also with tequila. Braddock had grimaced as the liquor sunk its fiery fangs into his flesh. Rojas had tied a folded bandana in place to serve as a crude bandage until Braddock could get some

RAVAGERS OF THE BORDER

real medical attention. He cleaned the wounds that the dun had suffered, as well, while Braddock held the horse's head and stroked its nose.

With that taken care of, they rode toward Chapparal City, taking the outlaws' horses with them. Braddock had Rosalita to his right and Rojas to his left. He asked Rojas, "How did you happen to run into señorita Ordóñez and her men?"

"Pure luck, I assure you, G.W. I had no idea they were following us. But when I told the señorita your name and said that you needed help, she was happy to volunteer the services of her vaqueros."

"My father's vaqueros," Rosalita corrected. "And do not get the swelled head, señor Braddock. I want answers, and I believed you might be able to provide them." She scowled. "Perhaps I would have been better off without them."

"The truth doesn't always turn out to be what we wish it was," Braddock said. "But I'm grateful to you, señorita, and you can believe that." He paused, then asked, "You did follow your brother from the ranch to Los Pinos, didn't you?"

For a moment, she didn't answer. Then, "Sí, I did. I wanted to find out why Javier had changed. Then I followed him across the border to Chapparal City. His actions were so odd, I had no idea what to make of them. But I had seen you there in Los Pinos, and after that in Chapparal City, and I thought you might be able to tell me what I wanted to know. So, when my men saw you being taken from the town, an obvious prisoner, along with this man, I followed again." She rode in silence, then added without looking at him, "I am glad we were able to prevent them from killing you, señor Braddock."

"So am I," said Braddock.

"Or should I say . . . Ranger Braddock?"

He shrugged. "You can just call me G.W., if you want," he said, not really answering the question.

Rosalita leaned forward slightly in the saddle and looked past Braddock at Rojas. "And what of you, señor?"

"What about me?" Rojas responded with a smile.

"Who are you, and why have you involved yourself in this affair?"

"Why, I am Francisco Rojas," he declared, pressing a hand flat to his chest. "Dashing young caballero who wishes to help my people and do battle against evil men."

"Did you really go to the university in St. Louis?" asked Braddock.

"Of course. I've never lied to you, G.W., except when I told you that my name was Chuco."

"You just didn't mention some of the truth."

Rojas shrugged. "Some say an omission is the same as a lie, some say it is not. I will leave others to debate such philosophical questions."

"You made it sound like you had a falling out with your father. What was that about?"

A frown creased Rojas's forehead. "That is something I am not prepared to discuss."

"Fine, have it your way. As long as you're on the right side."

"Of that you may be sure, my friend."

They rode on through the morning, the three of them trailed by the four vaqueros who had come with Rosalita from Rancho del Halcon. She had assured Braddock that they were fiercely devoted to their don's daughter, and so far he hadn't seen any reason to believe that wasn't so.

As they neared Chapparal City, Braddock reined in the dun and turned his head to look at Rosalita. "Why don't you and your vaqueros wait out here and let me and Francisco go in first?" he suggested.

She looked at him shrewdly. "So that if you encounter my brother and there is shooting, I won't be there to interfere?"

"Until we find out exactly what's going on, I just thought it might be easier on you to steer clear of things."

"Because even after everything that has happened, you don't completely trust that I won't take Javier's side."

"Can you give me your word that won't happen?"

Rosalita stared at him for a moment, then jerked her head toward the settlement visible in the distance. "Go ahead," she said. "But if I hear shots, I will come and see what is happening."

"Fair enough, I suppose," said Braddock. "If hell breaks loose, we'll probably need your help."

He nudged the dun into motion again and headed for Chapparal City with Rojas alongside him.

"Are we just going to ride in, bold as brass, G.W.?" Rojas asked.

"Not exactly. If Montayne's in town and spots us, he's liable to start blazing away at us. Alcazar probably wouldn't. He's maintained a pose as a respectable businessman, and more than likely he wants to keep that up until he gets what he wants, whatever that is. He could send gunmen after us if he saw us, though. I'd rather slip into town, see if we can get to the Alhambra, and maybe grab Alcazar before he knows we're anywhere around. If we're lucky, Javier Ordóñez will be there, and we can round him up, too."

Rojas nodded slowly while Braddock talked. Then he said, "So our theory is that Alcazar and this fellow Ordóñez are partners in the scheme."

"That fits all the facts and explains why Javier keeps turning up wherever there's trouble."

"And I believe it's correct. But what is their goal? As you put it, what are they after?"

Braddock shook his head. "That's still a mystery. But if we can get our hands on either or both of those hombres, maybe we can convince them to tell us."

"Considering that Alcazar ordered us thrown in that damned hole, I wouldn't mind getting the opportunity to question him."

Braddock couldn't argue with that sentiment.

They kept to the brush as much as possible as they approached the town, circling so that they could come at it from the south, where there were more storage buildings, barns, and corrals, and fewer people to notice them.

They tied the horses to some bushes behind a warehouse with no doors or windows in its rear wall. From there they worked their way deeper into the settlement, using what cover they could find. It was midday, but not a lot of people were moving around on the streets. Because of all the trouble during the past few months, Chapparal City wasn't as busy a place it had been before the border ravagers launched their raids. Too many folks had given up and left town, hoping for a fresh start elsewhere.

Braddock and Rojas took their time and eventually reached an alley next to a hardware store that gave them a decent view of the Alhambra. Some crates were stacked up next to the wall, providing cover for them as they watched the saloon. Braddock hoped they would spot Mauricio Alcazar coming or going from the place, but after they had been there a few minutes, it was Ed Montayne who appeared, pushing through the batwings and leaving the saloon. Braddock and Rojas pulled back so that the crates would conceal them better as Montayne crossed the street at an angle.

"He didn't see us, did he?" Rojas whispered.

"I don't think so."

"Where's he going?"

"Let's find out," Braddock said.

He edged around the front corner of the building, knowing that he was running a risk. Montayne could be walking right toward him.

Instead, the fair-haired outlaw was headed in the other direction, toward Patterson's Livery Stable. He went through the open double doors into the big building.

Braddock looked back at Rojas and called softly, "He went to the livery. Circle around back."

Rojas nodded his understanding and hurried away. Braddock walked along the street, well aware that he was out in the open and might be spotted by Alcazar or some other member of the gang. Maybe even by Javier Ordóñez if the young man was still in town. But he wanted to get his hands on Montayne, so he was willing to run the risk.

No one seemed to pay much attention to him, even with the bloodstained shirt he wore. As he approached the livery stable, his right hand hung near the butt of the Colt in his holster. It wasn't his regular gun—there was no telling what had happened to it while he was a prisoner—but it was the same model, one he had taken from a dead outlaw's hand. The Colt seemed to be in good working order.

Braddock eased up to the doors and heard the liveryman inside, saying, "—seen hide nor hair of 'em, mister. If you say they should've been back by now, I believe you, but I sure don't have any answers for you."

Braddock thought about it for a second and realized Montayne must have come in here to inquire about Dunlap and the other outlaws who had taken the two prisoners to the Devil's Hole. They'd had more than enough time to get there, dispose of Braddock and Rojas, and get back to Chapparal City. Alcazar had to be getting a little worried about them not showing up by now, so he had sent Montayne to make look into the matter.

"All right," Montayne said impatiently. "If you do see them—"

"He won't," Braddock said as he drew the Colt, stepped into the livery stable, and lined the gun's sights on Ed Montayne. "Nobody's ever going to see those sons of bitches again except the javelinas."

Montayne stiffened and his hand started toward the gun on his hip, but he froze as he peered over the barrel of Braddock's Colt into his eyes. Montayne must have realized how close he was to death at that moment.

"That's a wise move you just made," Rojas said as he came up behind Montayne and plucked the outlaw's gun from its holster. He had slipped in through the stable's rear door. "I'm sure G.W. wouldn't have minded killing you, even though we're hoping to make use of you. We could have always found some other way, though . . . and you *did* kill a friend of his."

"Edwards," Montayne practically spat. "That lying double-crosser."

"His name was John Edward Slattery," said Braddock. "And he was a better man than you'll ever be."

Patterson looked back and forth between the three of them and asked, "What in the sam hill is going on here?"

"This man's an outlaw," Braddock said, "and in the name of the State of Texas, he's under arrest."

He held out his left hand, cupping the Ranger badge

Rojas had returned to him. Official status or not, saying the words felt good. Mighty good.

"A Ranger," Patterson breathed.

"And I'm his loyal assistant," said Rojas. "Isn't that right, G.W.?"

"Right enough for now, I suppose," Braddock said. "We've got some questions for you, Montayne."

"You can go to hell," the outlaw replied defiantly. "I don't have to tell you anything, and I'm not going to."

"You don't have to answer, I suppose. But if you don't, you're no good to me . . . so here's what I'm thinking. There are plenty of people in Chapparal City you and your friends have hurt, Montayne. The town's dying because of you and your gang. So maybe what I'll do is turn you over to the people who are still here and let them deal with you." Braddock glanced at the liveryman, since Rojas was covering Montayne. "How does that sound to you, Mr. Patterson? Would you like to go and gather up some folks who might have a score to settle with the leader of the gang that's ruining your lives? Packy at the Red Top, maybe, and there are bound to be plenty of others."

Patterson said, "That sounds like a mighty interesting idea, Ranger. We could have ourselves a trial, and if this fella's the leader of that bunch, I reckon I know what the verdict would be . . . *and* the sentence we'd carry out."

"Wait a minute," Montayne blurted. "I'm not the leader. I just work for them. Alcazar and some greaser kid from below the border are behind the whole thing. They came up with the scheme, not me. I'm just a hired hand, like the others. Alcazar and the Ordóñez kid, they're the ones you want."

"Are they at the Alhambra?" asked Braddock.

"Alcazar is. The Mex rode out a while ago. I heard

him and Alcazar talking earlier about how it was time to get rid of his old man and his sister both, so he'd be running things down there." Now that Montayne had envisioned himself at the end of a hang rope, he couldn't get the words out fast enough. "He was going to gather up the men working for him on that side of the border and raid the ranch tonight. Finish the job."

That sent a chill through Braddock. He hadn't liked Javier Ordóñez, but for someone to be greedy and ambitious enough to wipe out his own family that way was just pure, snake-blooded evil.

Rojas looked like he felt the same way. "We have to stop them," he said.

"We will," Braddock said, "but first we need to round up Alcazar and any of his bunch left here in town. And there's one thing more I want to know, Montayne. What's behind all this?"

"What do you think?" said Montayne with a slight shake of his head, as if Braddock should have figured it out by now. "The railroad."

23

In the end, it was a fairly simple story of men lusting for wealth and power, as it so often was. Although it wasn't common knowledge yet, a railroad line was going to be extended to the Rio Grande valley. With a way to ship produce quickly enough that it would stay fresh until it reached its markets, and with the river itself to furnish water via irrigation, rich men were aiming to transform the valley on both sides of the border into an agricultural paradise and make themselves even bigger fortunes in the process.

Javier Ordóñez and Mauricio Alcazar, who had gotten wind of those plans somehow, wanted in on that windfall. They could make an even bigger profit by driving out all the landowners on both sides of the river, then buying up everything in sight at cheap prices.

Except for Rancho del Halcon. Javier would own that already, courtesy of the murders of his father and sister.

It was a hellish plan that Montayne laid out for Braddock and Rojas in the livery stable, with Patterson as a witness. "But here's the thing," the outlaw insisted when he was through. "I helped them put the thing together, but I never killed anybody myself."

"What about Slattery?"

Montayne shook his head. "The Ordóñez kid did that. He shot that other Ranger and then jumped you."

"You're a lying snake," Braddock said coldly, "and you're just trying to keep from getting your neck stretched. It won't work. The shots that killed Slattery came *after* Javier jumped me in the alley behind the place. Maybe you saved yourself from a rope today by cooperating with us, Montayne, but you're still going to hang."

Montayne drew in a deep, despairing breath, and then his shoulders slumped.

Braddock realized almost too late that Montayne's move was designed to slide a sleeve gun from a hidden spring holster into the palm of his hand. He jerked up the .41 caliber, two-shot derringer and fired.

But Braddock was already moving. He darted to the side and felt as much as heard the slug sizzling past his left ear. The Colt roared and bucked against his palm. Montayne twisted and rocked back as the bullet punched into his chest. His eyes widened in shock and pain, but he managed to stay on his feet as he tried to bring the derringer to bear for a second and final shot.

Rojas's gun blasted before Montayne was able to cock and fire. His bullet took the outlaw in the side of the head. Montayne crashed down, dead before he hit the dirt.

Patterson had stepped back quickly to get out of the line of fire. He stared at Montayne's bloody corpse for a second, then looked up at Braddock and Rojas.

"I'll testify that you shooting the fella was self-defense, if it ever comes to that," the liveryman said. "Don't reckon that's very likely, though."

"You heard everything he said about Alcazar and Javier Ordóñez, too," Braddock told him. "So, if anything happens to Francisco and me, you can explain to the law what it was all about."

"What are we going to do now?" asked Rojas as he replaced the cartridge he had just fired.

"Finish the round-up here in Chapparal City," Braddock replied grimly. "Alcazar's probably at the saloon." He thumbed a fresh round into his own gun. "And then we need to get señorita Rosalita and head for Rancho del Halcon as fast as we can, if we're going to get there in time to help her father."

BRADDOCK AND ROJAS walked out in the open now as they approached the Alhambra. There was no sign of Rosalita and the vaqueros with her, so Braddock figured they hadn't heard the shots a few minutes earlier. The report from Montayne's derringer hadn't been much more than a pop, and the livery stable's thick adobe walls would have muffled the shots from his and Rojas's Colts.

But the people in town had heard the shots and knew something was happening. They scurried for cover when they saw the guns Braddock and Rojas held. Whatever the trouble might be, it wasn't over yet.

One man stared at them with wide eyes and then turned to run toward the Alhambra. Braddock's gun came up. The man saw that and slammed on the brakes. He had hurrying to warn Alcazar, Braddock guessed, but he wasn't loyal enough to get shot over it. The man held up his hands, palms out, and shook his head vehemently as he backed off.

But as soon as Braddock and Rojas were past, he crouched and clawed at the holstered revolver on his hip.

Braddock saw that from the corner of his eye and whirled. The outlaw cleared leather, but that was all he accomplished before Braddock's gun thundered and a bullet flung him backward. The man hit the window of the business in front of which he stood and shattered it. Shards of glass sprayed out around him as he toppled out of sight.

Braddock and Rojas ran toward the Alhambra. Alerted by the shot, a man looked over the batwings, saw them, and yelled a warning. He jerked out a gun and fired. Braddock and Rojas both returned the shot. Their slugs smashed through the swinging doors and into the man's body, knocking him backward.

With a leap, Braddock went onto the boardwalk in front of the saloon. But instead of bulling through the batwings, he slid *under* them, feet first, taking the gunmen inside by surprise. A volley of shots struck the batwings and finished the job of blasting them into kindling, but the bullets all went over Braddock as he stretched out on the floor. His Colt swung swiftly from left to right with flame spurting from the muzzle.

He wasn't firing wildly, however, since he was aware that innocent folks could be in the saloon. The proof of that was in the way a number of men stampeded for the side door. The bartenders dived for cover behind the hardwood.

Each of Braddock's bullets found a man with a gun in his hand. As the outlaws crumpled under Braddock's deadly accurate fire, Rojas took advantage of the chance to charge into the saloon. He added his shots and two more outlaws fell.

A rifle cracked and a slug tore into the planks only inches from Braddock's head. He felt splinters sting his cheek. He rolled onto his belly, tipped his head back and his gun up, and fired at Mauricio Alcazar, who had appeared at the top of the staircase with a Winchester in his hands. Rojas threw a slug at Alcazar at the same time.

Both bullets ripped into the man's body. He bent forward from the impact and triggered the Winchester again, but this time the rifle bullet went into one of the stair treads below Alcazar. The Winchester slipped from his hands, which he pressed futilely to the blood-welling holes in his belly.

Then he toppled forward and rolled heavily down the stairs, coming to a stop in a limp, huddled heap at the bottom. As crimson pooled around him, it was obvious he was never going to move again.

Braddock pushed up onto one knee and then came to his feet next to Rojas. Rapid footsteps pounded outside. The two men turned quickly to see a group of towns-people bursting into the saloon, led by Patterson from the livery stable and Packy from the Red Top Café. The men held an assortment of pistols, rifles, and shotguns.

"We came to help you, Ranger," said Patterson, then added as he looked around the gunsmoke-hazed room, "but it looks like we got here a mite too late."

"Some of Alcazar's bunch may be just wounded," Braddock said. "You can take charge of them and fetch the undertaker for the others."

Patterson nodded. "We'll do that. What are you fellas fixin' to do?"

"We have one more bunch to stop," Braddock said, "but we'll have to head south of the border to do that."

THEY HAD JUST LEFT the saloon when Rosalita Ordóñez and the four vaqueros from Rancho del Halcon galloped up the street and skidded their mounts to a stop, causing dust to swirl up around them.

"Señor Braddock," Rosalita called. "We heard the shooting and came as quickly as we could, as I promised. What happened?"

"Alcazar and his bunch here in Chapparal City are done for," Braddock told her. "But before one of them died, he admitted to us that your brother and Alcazar were partners. He even said that Javier is the one who came up with the idea to run folks out of the valley."

"I don't believe it!"

Rojas said, "It's true, señorita. G.W. and I both heard him, and so did one of the citizens here in Chapparal City."

She stared at them, clearly upset at the idea of her own brother being so treacherous.

From the boardwalk in front of the Alhambra's main corner entrance, where he had just emerged in time to hear part of the conversation, Patterson said, "That's right, ma'am. I'm the one who heard that outlaw spill his guts." He held up a sheet of paper. "And this document we found upstairs in Alcazar's office lays out the reason behind the whole thing. The railroad's comin', and Alcazar and your brother figured to take over before it gets here."

"Madre de Dios," Rosalita murmured. She looked at Braddock. "It seems I must believe you."

"That's not the worst of it," he said. "Javier's headed back to Rancho del Halcon. He's going to round up the bandits who are working for him and raid the ranch again." Braddock's expression was grim. "From the sound of it, he plans to kill your father, and since he doesn't know that you're not there, I suspect that you're one of his targets, too."

"No!" she cried. "We must stop him!"

"Francisco and I are on our way to get our horses right now."

Patterson spoke up again, saying, "Why don't you take some extra mounts with you? You can make better time by swapping out, and I can furnish the horses if you need some besides those you brought in with you."

"Much obliged to you," Braddock said with a nod. "We'd best get riding!"

24

THE HORSES THEY HAD BEEN RIDING WERE TIRED ENOUGH that they took the time to switch their saddles over to fresh mounts before leaving Chapparal City, even though the delay chafed at Braddock.

He felt sorry for Rosalita, who was distraught at her brother's betrayal, but he intended to stop Javier despite that. John Edward Slattery and Juan Belmosa, along with countless others whose names Braddock didn't know, had died because of the young man's lawless quest for money and power. Javier Ordóñez had to be brought to justice . . . and G.W. Braddock was the man to do it.

They rode through the afternoon, stopping from time to time to rest the horses but otherwise moving at a ground-eating pace. When they reached the Rio Grande, they swapped the saddles back before splashing across the border river. That was past mid-afternoon.

"Should we go to Los Pinos, or head straight to the ranch?" Rojas asked Braddock. "We don't know how many men Javier will have with him when he attacks the place. We may not be enough to be a match for his force."

"What do you suggest?" asked Braddock. "You reckon we can get some help in Los Pinos?"

Rojas made a face and shook his head. "It's doubtful. If we just had more time . . . But we don't, so there's no point in wishing, is there? We should ride directly to the ranch and take our chances."

"Seems to be the only thing we can do," Braddock agreed with a nod.

"What are you two jabbering about?" Rosalita demanded. "We must get moving!"

Braddock figured her need for action was her way of coping with what her brother had done. He swung up into the saddle and said, "Lead the way, señorita. You probably know this country better than any of us."

Rosalita snorted and put her horse into a fast lope.

They continued riding toward Rancho del Halcon. The terrain on this side of the Rio Grande was a bit more rugged than that to the north, with a few ridges and shallow mesas visible in the fading light as the sun set and a golden dusk began to settle over the landscape. They were riding past one such mesa when a group of men on horseback suddenly surged out from behind it and surrounded them. Braddock and the other were forced to rein in as guns pointed at them from all sides.

Then booming laughter came from one of the men. He said, "Amigo! It is you again! What brings you back to Mexico?" The big man who had spoken moved his horse closer. "And in the company of such a lovely señorita as the beautiful Rosalita Ordóñez!"

Braddock said, "Bernal?"

The bandido thumped himself on the chest with a fist. "Sí, it is I, Valentín Bernal, the Lightning Bolt of Tamaulipas! Who else is that with you? He seems familiar—"

"A friend of mine named Francisco Rojas," replied Braddock, not wanting to take the time to explain that the last time Bernal had seen Rojas, the young *Tejano* had been pretending to be the lame beggar Chuco.

Bernal waved a hand and asked, "What are you doing here? Where are you going?"

Remembering everything Rojas had told him about Bernal, Braddock rolled the dice. "We're on our way to the Ordóñez rancho," he said. "We've found out the gang that's been operating along the border is going to raid the place tonight."

Bernal stared at him. "Es verdad?"

"It's true," Braddock assured the bandit leader. "They intend to kill Don Abraham, and we intend to stop them."

Bernal swept off his sombrero and executed a crude bow in the saddle to Rosalita. "I am sorry to hear of the trouble about to descend on your family, señorita," he declared. "If there is anything that Valentín Bernal, the Lightning Bolt of Tamaulipas, can do to assist you . . ."

Rosalita glanced over at Braddock and seemed to understand what he was thinking. Then she said to Bernal, "I am thankful to you, señor Bernal. We will be greatly outnumbered, and if you and your men could see fit to help us, I will be forever in your debt."

Bernal clapped his sombrero back on his head and waved a hand at his men. "Put those guns away!" he bellowed at them. "Can you not see that these are our amigos?" He turned back to Rosalita. "It would be our honor to assist you, señorita. For too long, these men have run roughshod over the border country. Now they must be stopped!"

"Gracias, señor Bernal. We have no time to waste—"

Bernal twisted in the saddle and gestured curtly to

his men once again. "Ride, you fools, ride! On to Rancho del Halcon!"

The whole group thundered westward.

Rojas moved his horse closer to Braddock and said, "Have you lost your mind, G.W.? These men are bandits. You can't trust them, especially Bernal."

"You just don't like him because he tried to kick you," Braddock replied with a faint smile. "I don't trust them, but I believe Bernal wants to eliminate any competition he has in these parts. And he's playing up to Rosalita."

"That won't do him any good."

"No, but as long as he thinks it might, I'm willing to have him on our side."

Rojas just shook his head as if he had lost all hope for Braddock's sanity.

Night closed in around them, but a big moon was already rising in the eastern sky behind them, casting a reddish-silver light over the landscape and giving it a bizarre appearance like Braddock imagined the surface of the moon might be like. The important thing was that it was bright enough for them to see where they were going so they could continue toward Rancho del Halcon.

Finally Rosalita said, "We're almost there—*Oh!*"

Her startled exclamation was prompted by the sound of gunfire drifting through the night air. Braddock looked ahead of them and saw pinpricks of light winking in the darkness. Muzzle flashes. A lot of them.

"Come on!" he called, his voice ringing with command. "The fight's already started!"

The riders plunged ahead, nineteen of them counting Bernal and his men. Within minutes, they were close enough to make out the buildings of the rancho's head-quarters. Gun flame stabbed all around the largest structure, the hacienda where Don Abraham lived. The raiders appeared to be laying siege to it.

"Spread out!" Braddock ordered his force. "Hit them hard and fast from all sides!"

"Do it, do it!" echoed Bernal, so his men would have no doubt whether to follow the Texan's commands.

Braddock's Colt was in his hand as he raced toward the hacienda. He figured that anybody outside the big house was one of Javier's raiders. The rancho's defenders would have withdrawn behind the adobe walls to make their stand.

He tried to keep track of Rojas and Rosalita, but as bullets began to fly around him like a swarm of hornets, that proved to be impossible. A man leaped out from behind a parked wagon and blazed away at him. Braddock aimed just below the muzzle flashes and triggered a shot. The man fell backward, throwing up his arms and howling in pain.

Another man stood up in the back of the wagon and opened fire with a rifle. Braddock's Colt boomed twice more as he flashed past on the dun. The rifleman pitched to the side and toppled over the wagon's sideboards.

Braddock hauled on the reins and pulled the dun into a tight turn. He was glad he was back on his old friend. Gunshots and the smell of powder smoke never spooked the dun. The horse was accustomed to such things.

Two men on foot charged at Braddock, firing. He sent the dun charging between them. The raiders had to leap apart to avoid being trampled. Braddock slammed a bullet into the man on his right. At the same time, he jerked his left foot from the stirrup and drove his boot heel into the face of the raider on that side. Even with all the chaos going on, he heard the sharp snap of the man's neck, like the sound of a tree branch breaking.

Braddock wheeled the dun again. Fewer gun flashes split the night now. The fight had been fierce but fast. As the shooting dwindled more, Rosalita cried, "Hold your fire! Hold your fire!"

Braddock was glad to hear that she was alive and sounded all right.

A few more shots boomed, then silence fell over the area around the hacienda. The heavy door in the wall opened and several men rushed out, their hands bristling with guns.

"Rosalita!" Don Abraham cried. "Rosalita, where are you?"

"Here, Papa!"

Braddock saw her swing down from her saddle where her horse was still moving and run to meet her father. Before they could reach each other, another figure on horseback swept between them.

"No!" Javier Ordóñez cried. "I won't be denied my destiny—"

Moonlight glinted on the gun in his hand as it swung toward his father. Rosalita stopped short, hesitated, then jerked her gun up.

Braddock fired before she could. The range was a little long, but he figured he could make the shot.

Javier threw up his arms and pitched from the saddle. The now riderless horse galloped on as Rosalita and Don Abraham were left standing with the sprawled figure of Javier lying on the ground between them.

Braddock dismounted and walked toward them, leading the dun. He held the Colt ready, but it didn't look like Javier was going to be moving again.

Rosalita turned to stare at him, her eyes big in the moonlight. "You . . . you . . ."

"I figure the whole thing will be hard enough for you

and your father without you having to pull that trigger," he said quietly.

Don Abraham dropped to his knees beside his son's body. "I . . . I don't understand," he said brokenly. "Javier. Javier . . ."

Rosalita whispered, "Gracias," to Braddock, then holstered her gun and went to her father. She bent, put her arm around his shoulders, and lifted him to his feet. She spoke softly to him as she led him away. Braddock couldn't hear what she was saying. It didn't matter. The words were between them.

Valentín Bernal swaggered up on Braddock's right. "It's over, eh?" he said. "All of those bandidos are dead. Are you wounded, amigo?"

"I'm fine," Braddock told him. "Thank you for your help."

"Dogs that come yapping around the feet of Valentín Bernal, the Lightning Bolt of Tamaulipas, will be kicked away, as they deserve." Bernal grinned. "And now, the beautiful señorita, she owes a debt to me, Valentín Bernal, the—"

"Will you *shut up?*" The angry question came from Rojas, who strode up on Braddock's left. "If you know what's good for you, you'll stay away from señorita Ordóñez, you . . . you bandit!"

"You!" Bernal stabbed his left forefinger toward Rojas. "I know you now!" He grabbed the gun on his hip.

Rojas drew at the same time, faster than Braddock had ever seen him pull a gun. In less than the blink of an eye, Rojas and Bernal had their Colts leveled at each other. Neither man squeezed the trigger, but the air was thick with the potential for more bloodshed.

As for Braddock, he had raised his gun, too, and had it pointed toward Bernal. Into the tense silence, he said,

"I still appreciate your help, mister, but you'd better put that gun down."

"But I know this man! I recognize him now."

"That's right," said Rojas. "I pretended to be a crippled beggar—"

"No, I mean I know who you *really* are," Bernal interrupted him. "A *teniente* of the Rurales! You were pointed out to me in Monterey!"

Braddock didn't take his eyes off Bernal, but it was Rojas he was addressing when he said, "You're a lieutenant in the Rurales? Well, that explains a few things. Reckon Slattery wasn't the only one working undercover."

"The Rurales are all thieves!" Bernal raged. "You are as big a bandit as me!"

"No, not all of us are bandits," Rojas said, his voice tight and angry. "Some of us still try to uphold the law. That means I should be arresting you, Bernal, and all of your bloody-handed cousins."

"Who just helped you beat this gang! What kind of gratitude is that?"

"I don't feel grateful to outlaws—"

Braddock said, "There are still quite a few more of them than there are of us, Francisco. Discretion might be the better part of valor here."

"You're quoting proverbs to me now, G.W.?"

"Just pointing out the obvious," said Braddock.

Rojas drew in a deep breath. "All right," he said. "I won't arrest you, Bernal."

"Oh, I am so thankful for that!" Bernal shot back at him with a sneer.

"But I'm warning you, stay away from Rancho del Halcon in the future. If I ever hear of you coming around here and bothering señorita Ordóñez, I'll hunt you down, I swear it."

"You frighten me." Still sneering, Bernal took a step back and lowered his gun slightly. "But because you were an ally, even for a short time, I will not kill you. I, Valentín Bernal, the Lightning Bolt of Tamaulipas, am famous for my generous spirit!" He slid the Colt back into leather and then pointed at Rojas again. "But there will be another day and another meeting for us . . . Chuco!"

"Just go," Rojas said through clenched teeth.

Bernal squared his shoulders, turned his back defiantly, and sauntered off, calling to his men. A minute later, they all galloped off into the night.

Braddock and Rojas didn't pouch their irons until the bandits were gone. Braddock started to say something, but Rojas interrupted him.

"Please, G.W. We've both accomplished our goals. The border will be a safer place to live now, at least for a while."

Braddock wasn't going to let it go that easily. He said, "That falling out with your father, it was over you joining up with the Rurales, wasn't it?"

"He said we were Texans, and that the Rurales were all bandits, just like Bernal said. But I wanted to prove to him that he was wrong." Rojas shrugged. "Time will tell." He inclined his head toward the hacienda. "You should go on in. I'm sure the señorita is grief-stricken right now, but in time she will be grateful to you for everything you've done."

"Not me," Braddock said. "I'll leave that to you." He put a foot in the stirrup and swung up onto the dun. "I'm going home."

"Back to Texas, you mean?"

"Not anymore," Braddock said. He turned and rode into the night, seeing in his mind's eye the trail laid out before him, the trail to Esperanza, the closest thing to a home he had these days, where he would wait patiently until Texas once more had a need for an outlaw Ranger.

AUTHOR'S NOTE

In 1904, the railroad did come to the lower Rio Grande valley and joined forces with the growing practice of irrigation to make agriculture the dominant activity in the region. Many small ranchers—Texan, *Tejano*, and Mexican—on both sides of the border saw their spreads gobbled up by wealthy businessmen. Some of those ranches had been in the same families for generations. It was a time of turmoil, but the events in this novel are fictitious, purely the product of the author's imagination.

Likewise, there are several geographical features in Texas known as the Devil's Hole, the Devil's Sinkhole, and the Devil's Waterhole, but the one in this novel doesn't exist. Like everything else, I made it up.

TAKE A LOOK RATTLER'S LAW: VOLUME ONE

WHEN WAR ERUPTS OVER MOONSHINE, BLOOD IS SPILLED ALONG WITH WHISKEY!

Wild Bill Hickok may be gone, but Abilene is still a wild and woolly cow town in need of a strong marshal to bring law and order to its streets. That man is Lucas Flint . . . a legendary lawman sometimes known as the Rattler because of his swift and deadly speed with a Colt .45. Together with his deputy, dashing young gunfighter Cully Markham, Lucas Flint will take on any challenge that threatens the safety of the town and its people that he's sworn to protect.

In this first collection of Rattler's Law novels, Flint and Cody battle a ruthless criminal overlord who has taken over the town. A traveling circus visits Abilene, bringing with it unexpected danger. Cully finds himself at the head of a posse tracking down a gang of train robbers. Settlers want only a new place to make their homes, but a violent band of masked marauders has another idea. A half-Kiowa army scout visits Abilene, unaware that a renegade war party is on his trail. Lucas Flint travels to Wyoming to solve a murder and save an innocent woman from the gallows. Big-city criminals show up in Abilene intent on killing a famous pugilist.

Rattler's Law, Volume One includes: The Town Tamer, Deadeye, The Train Robbers, Rancher's Revenge, Out for Blood, Shadow of the Gallows, A Solid Right Cross, and Whiskey Trail.

AVAILABLE NOW

ABOUT THE AUTHOR

James Reasoner has been telling tales and spinning yarns as far back as he can remember. He's been doing it professionally for more than 40 years, and during that time, under his own name and dozens of pseudonyms, he's written almost 400 novels and more than 100 shorter pieces of fiction. His books have appeared on the *New York Times, USA Today,* and *Publishers Weekly* bestseller lists. He has written Westerns, mysteries, historical sagas, war novels, science fiction and fantasy, and horror fiction.

Growing up in the late Fifties and early Sixties when every other series on television was a Western made him into a lifelong fan of the genre. The Lone Ranger, Roy Rogers, Hopalong Cassidy, Matt Dillon, and John Wayne made quite an impression on him. At the age of 10, he discovered Western novels when he checked out *Single Jack* by Max Brand and *Hopalong Cassidy* (there's that name again!) by Clarence E. Mulford from the library bookmobile that came out every Saturday to the small town in Texas where he lived. He's been reading Westerns ever since, long before he started writing them, and always will.

James Reasoner has also written numerous articles, essays, and book introductions on a variety of topics related to popular culture, including vintage paperbacks and the publishing industry, pulp magazines, comics, movies, and TV. He writes the popular blog *Rough*

Edges and is the founder and moderator of an email group devoted to Western pulp magazines.

He lives in the same small town in Texas where he grew up and is married to the popular mystery novelist Livia J. Washburn, who has also written Westerns under the name L.J. Washburn.

Printed in Great Britain
by Amazon